The Little Amish Matchmaker

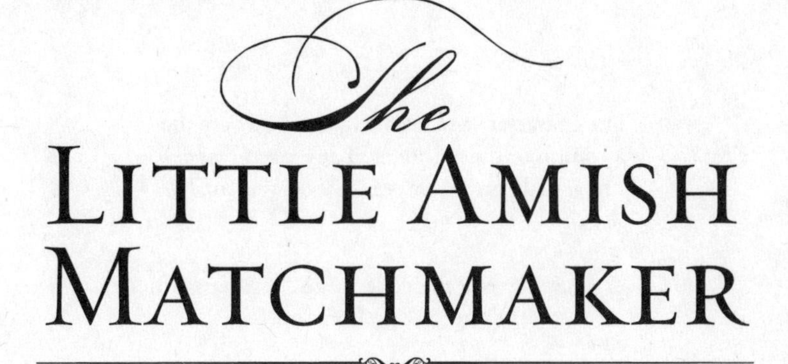

The Little Amish Matchmaker

A Christmas Romance

Linda Byler

Intercourse, PA 17534
800/762-7171
www.GoodBooks.com

The characters and events in this book are the creation of the author, and any resemblance to actual persons or events is coincidental.

Cover design by Koechel Peterson & Associates, Inc., Minneapolis, Minnesota

Design by Cliff Snyder

THE LITTLE AMISH MATCHMAKER

International Standard Book Number: 978-1-56148-776-9
Library of Congress Control Number: 2012941923

Publisher's Cataloging-in-Publication Data

Byler, Linda.
The little Amish matchmaker : a Christmas romance / Linda Byler.
p. cm.
ISBN 978-1-56148-776-9

1. Amish --Fiction. 2. Teachers --Fiction. 3. Courtship --Fiction.
4. Christmas stories. 5. Christian fiction. 6. Love stories. I. Title.

PZ7.B9882 Li 2012
[Fic] --dc23 2012941923

Table of Contents

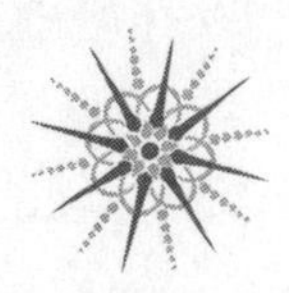

Chapter One

He gripped the handlebar of his fleet red scooter with one hand, reached up and smashed his straw hat down on his thick brown hair as far as it would go, hunkered down and prepared for the ascent.

Traverse Hill was no child's play, he knew. You had to stay sharp. Especially this morning, with the fine, hard snow just starting to drive in from the northeast, pinging against his face like midget cannonballs. They hurt.

His ears were two red lumps of ice. That was what happened if you didn't wear a beanie to school, but Dat frowned on them, saying he never wore one. In his day, you wore your Amish hat to go to school, not a beanie, which in his view, was still the law, or *ordnung*, of the church.

He said this in the same level way he said everything: that half smile, the gentleness, the genuine kindness that was always in his voice.

Isaac had never heard Dat raise his voice in anger. He was firm, but always kind. *Ordnung* mattered to him. His family was raised to be conservative, strictly adhering to the old ways, never judging others who were less stringent.

Isaac thought Dat was a lot like God. He wanted your obedience, but it came easy, being loved the way Isaac was.

Sometimes, Isaac would have liked to have a beanie, or a red shirt that had faint stripes in it, or a pair of suspenders with prints on them, gray or navy blue or red. But it was not Dat's way. Or Mam's for that matter.

Mam was a lot like Dat, only she talked too much. She said the same thing over and over, which usually drove Isaac a little crazy, but Mam was just busy being Mam.

When Mam milked the cows, she lifted those heavy milkers as handily as Dat, her red men's kerchief tied the whole way over her brown hair, her cheeks round and flushed, her green eyes snapping, always whistling or singing or talking.

Isaac's eyes were green, like Mam's. His last name was Stoltzfus, and he lived in Lancaster County, where a bunch of Amish people lived, making up a large community of plain folks, all members of the Old Order. Isaac was the youngest son in a family of 10 children. All of them were baptized, the older ones married in the Amish church. Seven sisters and two brothers.

Jonas got married to Priscilla a year ago in December. Mam said wasn't that the most wonderful thing, attending your son's wedding, being the guest of honor and not having to do a single, solitary thing all day except eat and sing German hymns, which, after talking, was Mam's favorite thing to do.

The other Stoltzfus brother, Simon, was still at home. He was 21, and worked with Dat on the farm. The German version of Simon's name was "Sim," or "Simmy," but since he was older, they called him Sim. He was already a member of the church, so he was never very disobedient.

Isaac was in seventh grade, attending Hickory Grove School, a one-room parochial school nestled in a grove of maple trees on the edge of Leroy Zook's farm. There were 22 pupils. The teacher's name was Catherine Speicher, and she was about the prettiest, sweetest girl he had ever met.

Isaac didn't think girls were of much account. Not one of them had any common sense. They shrieked hysterically about nothing and sniffed in the most annoying manner when you traded arithmetic papers to check in class. They sniffed because they were mad that they had more wrong than he did. But they weren't allowed to say anything, so they drew air in through their noses and batted their eyelashes, giving their faces something to do if they weren't allowed to speak.

Girls were all the same, in Isaac's opinion.

Except this new teacher, Catherine Speicher. She could stay quiet. Common sense rested on her shoulders, and she wore it like a fine cape. She was excellent with those squirmy little first-graders. Isaac had to be careful or he'd get carried away, watching her animated face as she explained letters and numbers to the little ones.

She was fancy, in a way. She wore bright colors and combed her blond hair a bit straighter, not rolled in as sleekly as his Mam or all his married sisters. Her eyes were so blue he thought they could be artificial, but Dat said those Speichers all had blue eyes, so he guessed they were the real thing. She was also kind, like Dat.

You could hardly disobey Dat and feel right about it. That was why Isaac wore his straw hat on weekday winter mornings. Dat was very frugal. Straw hats didn't cost as much as black felt hats, so his and Mam's boys wore straw hats, even in winter, except for more important times like church and funerals and maybe school Christmas programs.

Isaac's plastic Rubbermaid lunch box rattled in the wire basket attached to his handlebars, and the wind whistled in his cold ears. The front brim of his hat jigged up and down. He closed his eyes to mere slits, enough to watch where he was going but nothing much besides. As he swooped to the bottom of the hill, his pace slowed, and he saw the dark forms of his classmates arriving from each direction.

The schoolhouse was hunkered down under the maple trees, its yellowish stucco walls withstanding the snow and cold, the same as it always had. There were paper candy canes and holly on the windows, the red and green colors looking so much like Christmas, especially now that it was snowing this morning. The Christmas program was only a month away, which sent little knots of excitement dancing in his stomach. School programs were nerve-wracking.

"Hey, Professor!" Calvin Beiler waved from his scooter, his gray beanie pulled low over his ears.

"Morning, Calvin!" Isaac yelled back.

Isaac was used to being called "Professor." It started as a joke, when he was fitted with a pair of eyeglasses, Mam taking him to Lancaster City to an eye specialist when he had trouble seeing the blackboard. His glasses were sturdy but plain, a bit rounder than he would have liked, but Mam said they were serviceable, strong and very expensive, meaning he had better be careful with them.

So because Isaac could multiply in his head, recite the Beatitudes in German, say "The Village Blacksmith" without missing a word ever since he was in fourth grade and was always at the top of his class, they started calling him "Professor."

He was secretly pleased.

He had found out early on you couldn't brag about it. That simply didn't work. You kept your mouth shut about your grades, learned to praise others and then everyone liked you.

"Didn't your ears freeze coming down that hill?"

"Oh, they're cold." Isaac grinned, rubbing them with his gloved hands.

Calvin grinned back, and nothing more was said. It was okay. Calvin's parents were more liberal, allowing more stylish things like different colored sneakers with white on them, which looked really sharp. But somehow it never bothered either of them that Isaac wore black sneakers, plain all over. They just liked each other a lot.

They both loved baseball, fishing and driving ponies. Calvin's parents raised miniature ponies, but he had a Shetland pony named Streak that was the color of oatmeal with a caramel-colored mane and tail.

Isaac had four ponies. He was very good with the ponies, Dat said, but only Calvin knew about Dat saying that, because it would be bragging to tell anyone else.

Best friends knew you through and through. You didn't have to be afraid of anything at all.

Whatever you said or did was acceptable, and if it wasn't, then Calvin would say so, which was also acceptable. Or the other way around.

Like trading food. Isaac's Mam raised huge neck pumpkins, not the round orange kind that everyone thinks of when you say pumpkin. Neck pumpkins were greenish brown, or butterscotch-colored, shaped like a huge gourd. Or a duck or goose.

Mam tapped them, picked them, peeled and cooked them. Then she cold-packed the mounds of orange pumpkin, set the jars away in the canning cellar and made the best, custardy, shivery-high pumpkin pies anyone ever had.

Calvin would trade the entire contents of his lunch box for one large slice of that pie. Isaac never took it, of course, just taking one of Calvin's chocolate Tastycakes, those little packages of cupcakes Mam would never buy. Or his potato chips, and sometimes both. Then if Calvin got too hungry at last recess, Isaac would share his saltines with peanut butter and marshmallow cream.

When the bell rang, Teacher Catherine stood by the bell pull inside the front door, smiling, nodding, saying good morning. She was wearing a royal-blue dress and cape, her black apron pinned low on her waist. Her white covering was a bit heart-shaped and lay on her ears, the strings tied in a loose bow on the front of her cape.

Her cheeks were a high color, a testimony to her own cold walk to school, probably shouldering that huge, green backpack like always.

Isaac hung up his homemade black coat, putting his hat on the shelf. He ran his fingers through his thick hair, shook his head to settle it away from his forehead and slid into his desk.

Ruthie Allgyer slid into hers across the aisle, never turning her head once to acknowledge his presence.

Fine with me, Isaac cast a sidelong glance in her direction. He decided anew that girls were an unhandy lot. There she was, her eyebrows lifted with anxiety, a tiny mirror already held to her face as she scraped at a gross-looking pimple with a fingernail.

Yuck. He swallowed, looked away.

"Good morning, boys and girls!"

"Good morning, Teacher!"

The chorus from the mouths of 22 children was a benediction for Teacher Catherine, who glowed as if there was a small sun somewhere in her face, then bent her blond head to begin reading a chapter of the Bible. Her voice was low, strong and steady, pronouncing even "Leviticus" right. His teacher was a wonder.

Ruthie sniffed, coughed, stuck her whole head into her desk to find a small package of Kleenexes, extracted one after a huge rumpus, then blew her nose with the most horrendous wet rattle he had ever heard.

Isaac winced, concentrating on the Bible story.

They rose, recited the Lord's Prayer in English, then sang a fast-paced good morning song as they all streamed to the front of the classroom, picking up the homemade songbooks as they passed the stack.

Ruthie stood beside Isaac, so he had to share a songbook. She was still digging around with that dubious Kleenex, snorting and honking dry little sounds of pure annoyance, so he leaned to the right as far as he could and held the songbook with thumb and forefinger.

His shoulder bumped against Hannah Fisher's, and she glared self-righteously straight into his eyes, so he hove to the left only a smidgen, stood on his tiptoes and stared straight up to the ceiling, the only safe place.

He certainly hoped girls would change in the next 10 years, or he'd never be able to get married. Girls like Teacher Catherine only came along once in about 20 years, he reasoned.

He had a strong suspicion his brother Sim was completely aware of this as well.

For one thing, Sim had offered to bring the gang mower to mow the schoolyard back in

August. A gang mower was a bunch of reel mowers attached to a cart with a seat on it, and shafts to hitch a horse into. It was the Amish alternative to a gas-powered riding mower, and a huge nuisance, in Isaac's opinion. By the time you caught a horse in the pasture and put the harness and bridle on him, you could have mowed half the grass with an ordinary reel mower. Isaac had caught Sim currycombing his best Haflinger, Jude, the prancy one. Then Sim gave Isaac the dumbest answer ever when he asked why he was hitching Jude to the gang mower instead of Dolly, who was far more dependable.

Besides using Jude, Sim had showered and then dressed in a sky-blue Sunday shirt which, to Isaac's way of thinking, was totally uncalled for.

He even used cologne. Now if that wasn't a sure sign that you noticed someone, Isaac didn't know what was.

It was a wonder he hadn't taken a rag to the mower blades. Polished them up.

Sim stayed till dark, even. Got himself a drink at the hydrant by the porch when Catherine was sweeping the soapy water across the cement, just so he could say hello to her.

Isaac was going to have to talk to Sim, see if he could arrange something.

That whole scenario had been way back before school started, when all the parents came to scrub and scour, wax the tile floor, mow and trim the schoolyard, paint the fence, repair anything broken, all in preparation for the coming term.

They wouldn't have had to use the gang mower. Weed-eaters did a terrific job, especially if 10 or 11 of them whined away at once.

But Isaac supposed if you wanted attention from a pretty teacher, a prancing Haflinger and a blue shirt would help.

Before they began arithmetic class, Teacher Catherine announced she had all the copies ready for the Christmas program. Amid excited ooh's, quiet hand-clapping, and bouncing scholars in their seats, she began by handing the upper-graders their copies of the Christmas plays.

Isaac's heart began a steady, dull acceleration, as if he was running uphill with his scooter.

Would he be in a play?

Oh, he hoped. There was nothing in all the world he loved more than being in a Christmas play. He was as tall as the eighth-grade boys. Almost, anyway. Sim was tall. He was over six feet, with green eyes and dark skin. Isaac thought he looked a lot like Sim, only a bit better around the nose.

Sure enough. A fairly thick packet was plopped on his desk.

"Isaac, do you think you can carry the main part of this play, being Mr. Abraham Lincoln? Ruthie will be Mrs. Lincoln."

Isaac looked up at Teacher Catherine, met those blue eyes and knew he would do anything for her, even have Ruthie as his wife in the Christmas play. When Catherine smiled and patted his shoulder, he smiled back, nodded his head and was so happy he could have turned cartwheels the whole way up the aisle to the blackboard.

Yes, he would have to talk to Sim.

Chapter Two

OUTSIDE, THE SNOW KEPT DRIVING AGAINST the buildings, the red barn standing like a sentry, guarding the white house, the round, tin-roofed corn crib and the red implement shed on the Samuel Stoltzfus farm.

Darkness had fallen, so the yellow lantern light shone in perfect yellow squares through the swirling snow, beacons of warmth and companionship. A large gray tomcat took majestic leaps through the drifts, making his way to the dairy barn where he knew a warm dish of milk would eventually be placed in front of him.

Heifers bawled, impatiently awaiting their allotment of pungent corn silage.

The Belgian workhorses clattered the chains attached to their thick leather halters, tossing their heads in anticipation as Isaac dug the granite bucket into the feed bin.

A bale of hay bounced down from the ceiling, immediately followed by another. Then a pair of brown boots and two sturdy legs followed, and Sim pounced like a cat, grabbing Isaac's shoulder.

"Gotcha!"

"You think you're scary? You're not." Isaac emptied the bucket of grain into Pet's box, then turned to face Sim. "Hey, why don't you ask Teacher Catherine for a date?"

No use beating around the bush, mincing words, hedging around, whatever you wanted to call it. Eventually, you'd have to say those words, so you may as well put them out there right away. Sort of like that gluey, slimy, toy stuff you threw against a wall and it stuck, then slowly climbed down, after you watched it hang on the wall for awhile.

The long silence that followed proved that Sim had heard his words. All the lime-green fluorescence of them.

Isaac hid a wide grin, shouldered another bucket of feed, calmly dumped it into Dan's wooden box, then turned and faced Sim squarely. In the dim light of the hissing gas lantern, swinging from the cast-iron hook that had hung there for generations, he was surprised to find Sim looking as if he was going to be sick.

Sim's face was whitish-green, his mouth hung open and he looked a lot like the bluegills did after you extracted the hook from their mouths and threw them on the green grass of the pond bank. Even his eyes were bulging.

"What's the matter?"

Sim closed his mouth, then opened it, but no words came out.

"Nothing can be that bad," Isaac said over his shoulder as he went to fill a bucket for Sam.

"Why in the world would I do something like that? In a thousand years she would never take me."

Isaac had no idea Sim was as spineless as that. Why couldn't he just approach her and ask? If she said no, then that was that. No harm done. At least he had tried.

"You think so?" is what Isaac said instead.

"Yes." Sim jerked his head up and down. "What would a girl like her want with ... well, me? She's way above my class."

That was stupid. "There is no such thing as class. Not for me and Calvin."

"Well, there is for me." Sim reached out and tipped Isaac's straw hat. "I live in the real world. I know when I have a chance and when I don't."

Isaac bent over and picked up his hat, stuck it on top of his head, then smashed it down firmly. It felt right. That tight band around his head, just above his eyes, was a part of him, like breathing and laughing. His hat shaded the sun, kept angry bumblebees from attacking his hair, kept the rain and snow off, and if he wore it at a rakish angle, it made him look like an eighth-grader.

"Did you ask God for her? The way Mam says?" Isaac asked.

Sim dug in his pocket for his Barlow knife. He found it and flicked it open before bending to cut the baling twine around a bale of hay. "It's not right to ask God for a million dollars or a mansion or something to make you happy."

"Who said?"

Isaac leaned against the hand-hewn post, tipped back his straw hat, stuck a long piece of hay in his mouth and chewed solemnly.

"But the thing is, you don't know. If it's God's will for your life, he might consider it."

Sim shook his head, mumbled something.

"What did you say?"

"Nothing you'd understand."

"Are you coming to the Christmas program?" Isaac asked.

"When is it?"

Isaac shrugged. "You could offer to fix the front door before then."

"Look, Ikey, give it up. She'd—"

"Stop calling me Ikey!"

"She'd never consider me. She's … just too … pretty and classy and awesome. Besides, she was dating Rube King."

Isaac lifted a finger, held it aloft. "Was! There's the word. Was!"

"Well, if she'd say yes, it would soon be a 'was!'"

Isaac knew defeat when he saw it, so he went to help Mam with the milking. He was cold and sleepy. He wished chores were finished so he could go indoors and curl up on the couch with his Christmas play.

The cow stable was pungent, steamy and filled with the steady "chucka-chucka" sound of four, large, stainless-steel milkers extracting the milk from the sturdy, black and white Holsteins. His mother was bent beside a cow, wiping the udder with a purple cloth dipped in a disinfecting solution. She straightened with a grunt, smiled at him and asked if his chores were finished.

"The chickens yet."

"You might need a snow shovel. It was drifting around the door this afternoon already."

Isaac nodded and then bent his head, prepared to meet the onslaught awaiting him the minute he opened the cow-stable door. It did no good. A gigantic puff of wind clutched his hat and sent it spinning off into the icy, whirling darkness. He felt his hair stand straight up, then whip to the left, twisting to the right. No use looking for his hat now. He had better take care of the chickens.

Isaac's heart sank when he saw the snowdrift. No way could he get into that chicken house without shoveling. He retraced his steps, found the shovel and met the cold head-on once more. His ears stung painfully as his hair tossed about wildly. This was no ordinary snowstorm; it was more like a blizzard. Likely there would be no school tomorrow.

He was able to wedge his way into the chicken house through the small opening, quickly opening the water hydrant and scattering laying mash into the long, tin trough. He fluffed up the dry shavings the hens had thrown in the corner. Then Isaac made a headlong dive out of the warmth of the henhouse, wading through knee-high snow to the house.

He was surprised to see Dat on the front porch, kicking snow off his chore boots.

"You done already?" he asked his father.

"No, Sim's finishing. Levi Beiler came over, riding his horse. They need help at the Speicher home."

"Speicher? Teacher Catherine?"

Dat nodded soberly.

"What happened?"

"I'm not sure."

That sort of answer was no answer at all, but Isaac knew it meant he did not need to know, that he should go into the house and ask no questions. When Dat laid a reassuring hand on his shoulder and Isaac looked up, Dat's eyes were warm in the light from the kitchen.

"You think you'll ever find your hat?"

Dat's hand spread a whole new warmth through him, a comfort, an understanding.

"I have another one. My school hat." He fixed himself a large saucepan of Mam's homemade hot cocoa mix and milk. The whole saucepanful ran over, hissing and bubbling into the burner, turning the blue gas flame orange. Isaac jumped up and flipped the burner off, salvaging his warm drink. He dumped the hot cocoa into a mug that said Snoopy on it. Mam loved yard sales. She had a whole collection of funny mugs which made Dat smile.

Mam came in, went to the wash house and kicked around to get her boots off, all to the tune of "God Rest Ye Merry Gentlemen."

He was proud of Mam. She was one smart lady. Not very many Amish people knew that song, but she did. She knew lots of things. She knew what Orthodox Jews were, and synagogues, and she knew who the leader of Cuba was. She explained dictatorship to Isaac, and Dat hid his head behind the *Botschaft* for a long time when Isaac said his teacher was a dictator. That, of course, was before Catherine Speicher.

He wrapped both hands around the Snoopy mug of hot cocoa, took a sip and burned his tongue.

Mam came through the door, taking off her apron, sniffing and asking what was burning.

"The cocoa ran over."

Mam frowned. She hurried to the stove, peered at the blackened burner, and then bent for her tall green container of Comet. "Tsk, tsk. Should have wiped it off, Ikey. This is quite a blizzard. There are no cars moving at all. The snowplow is going, though, so I'm sure they'll keep some of the roads open."

Mam was basically doing what she did best, talking. No matter if Isaac didn't reply, she rattled on anyway. "Sim went with Dat. They're having trouble with their water pump. At least that's what I thought he said. Don't know why Sim had to go. You'd think Dat and Abner could handle it. Well, see, they can't run out of water. Those calves and heifers they raise need water. Isaac, what are you reading? School stuff? Christmas plays, I bet. You know I'm not allowed to see it. Just tell me the title. Is it a play? Are you hungry? I'm going to eat a chocolate whoopie pie. I made them this afternoon. You want one to dip in your cocoa? Better not dip it. Whoopie pies fall apart, they're so soft."

By the time she reached the pantry, she was singing again, partly under her breath, a sort of humming with words. She was carrying a large rectangular Tupperware container with a gold-colored lid, one Isaac knew contained either whoopie pies or chocolate chip cookies. Sometimes she made pumpkin or oatmeal whoopie pies, but she always had to put some of them in the freezer for sister's day. Her boys just weren't so *schlim* (fond of) pumpkin or oatmeal.

"Guess none of these will last for sister's day, huh?" Mam said, as she kept talking while pouring herself a glass of creamy milk. Isaac raised his eyebrows, knowing Mam wouldn't expect an answer.

Sister's day was a regularly occurring hazard, in his opinion. First of all were those 18 nieces and nephews to contend with. All his Legos, model ships, harmonicas and BB guns had to be stowed into hiding. His sisters sat around the table and ate, drank endless quantities of coffee, discussed either people or food and didn't watch their offspring one bit.

Especially Bennie. That little guy could do with a good paddling from his dat, not his mam. Isaac told him a dozen times to leave that wooden duck decoy alone, the one that sat on his chest of drawers, but inevitably Bennie would climb up on his bed, then his clothes hamper, and get that decoy down. Every time. Isaac told Mam, which did absolutely no good. Mam's head was stuffed full of babies and recipes and songs and time on the clock and all kinds of troubles. Some things in life you were better off shutting your mouth about and not caring so much. It was only a wooden duck.

But if Bennie ran with the wild crowd in his *rumspringa* years, they couldn't say they hadn't been warned. He'd done his best.

He yawned, rubbed his eyes, then reached for a whoopie pie. Slowly, he dug at the Saran Wrap, uncovering half of it, then sank his teeth into the chocolatey goodness.

"Better get in the shower. Be sure and brush your teeth. Don't forget to brush for a whole minute," Mam called.

That, too, was a ridiculous thing. If you brushed your teeth for 60 seconds, you ended up swallowing all the toothpaste, which could not be good for your digestive system. So he never timed himself, just brushed awhile.

Isaac's last thought was wondering what was going on at the Speichers before he fell asleep.

Chapter Three

IT WAS UNBELIEVABLE, BUT IN THE MORNING, the light was still gray, the air stinging with brutish, icy snow. They did the chores swiftly, shoveling drifts from doorways, opening frozen water pipes with propane torches.

No school, of course, although Isaac knew they could have, so it would be a sort of holiday. Horses pulling a carriage or sleigh could get through deep snow, but most horses were terrified of snowplows. With this amount still coming down, those clattering monsters with yellow blinking lights and chains rattling would be plowing the drifting snow back into place. It was better to take the day off.

Isaac never found out when Sim came home, and he didn't bother asking about the trouble at the Speichers. Sim was a puzzle. His eyes were way too bright, almost feverish, and yet he looked completely miserable. Isaac figured he'd have all day to corner Sim, which he fully intended to do.

Mam made fried cornmeal mush, stewed crackers, puddin's and fried eggs for breakfast.

"*Mush und levva vosht.* (Mush and puddin's) Nothing better on a cold winter day," Dat said, gazing warmly at Mam. Her cheeks flushed like red apples as she basked in his praise.

Isaac squirted homemade ketchup all over his stewed crackers, then cut a bit of fried egg and laid it on top. Shoveling it onto his fork, he wedged it into his mouth, then bit off a corner of his toast spread with homemade raspberry jelly and watched Sim's face.

Seriously, that poor guy was in a bad way. He didn't even talk.

Dat opened the subject, saying Abner Speicher was taken to the hospital, with a bad case of pneumonia, only worse. He wasn't sure what it was; viral something. A few hours later their water pump gave out, leaving the calves in the veal barn without water.

Dat hated gossip. He never belittled anyone, but Isaac could see he was choosing his words carefully, trying hard not to disparage his neighbor. Not everyone had the same work ethic as Dat, nor owned three farms. Dat was very humble in that respect, teaching his sons to never speak of the farms he possessed.

He asked Sim if they wanted to have a working day at the Speichers, sort of a frolic.

When Sim choked on his mush and had to swallow some juice, then choked on the acidic drink, Isaac burst out laughing uproariously. Sim smacked his arm, but Isaac kept on laughing.

Dat and Mam were clueless, the expressions on

their faces much the same as the duck decoy on his chest of drawers.

While their parents drank their coffee, Isaac and Sim went to the basement for some cider. As soon as they were out of earshot, Isaac crowed triumphantly. "Do you think you should have a frolic at the Speichers?" then scampered behind the Ping-Pong table before Sim could catch him.

Sim shook his head, telling him he was too big for his britches.

"Did she help you fix the water pump?"

"No."

"Did you go into the house?"

"Yes."

"Did you see her?"

"Yes."

"Did you talk to her?"

"Of course not. Her mother made coffee and set out some kind of cupcakes."

"Did you eat one?"

Without answering, Sim asked, "Is Catherine shy?"

"No. Not one bit. She's just right."

That was the end of the conversation. Sim would not say one more word, taking the jar of home-canned cider upstairs and heating it, his thoughts clearly a million miles away.

They hitched Pet and Dan to the bobsled, that ancient, hazardous rattletrap half hidden in the haymow with loose hay and cobwebs. They swept the bobsled clean, rubbed it with moist old cloths, spread clean straw on the bed, oiled the runners and springs, fixed the seat with two extra screws, then settled bales of hay covered with buggy blankets behind the front seat.

Isaac was allowed to wear one of Sim's beanies, Dat saying a storm like this was a rare and wonderful thing, but not to expect to wear one always. They were worldly, in his opinion, but you needed to exercise common sense on a day like this.

Isaac couldn't express his feeling of absolute happiness, sitting up there beside Sim, wearing the beanie he wore to play hockey. He felt like a true king reigning over his subjects. Not one thing could go wrong.

Pet and Dan were both the same color, a light caramel with lighter manes and tails. They were brushed to sleek perfection, the black well-oiled harness slapping against their rounded haunches as they broke into a heavy, clumsy trot, their hooves making a dull "thok-thoking" sound against the snow. Their manes were so heavy they broke apart on top of their massive necks, then jiggled back and forth with each step.

It was snowing still. Isaac bent his head to avoid the stinging flakes, but after a few miles he became used to it. They picked up Calvin and his sister Martha and gave them a ride, making a wide circle before depositing them on their driveway again. They picked up some chicken feed at the hardware store in Bird-In-Hand, then turned to go back home.

Isaac was checking out the new sign in front of the bakery when he heard Sim yell, "Whoa!"

He turned to look down into the astonished eyes of his teacher.

"Do you need a ride?"

In disbelief, Isaac watched as his beloved teacher's eyes filled with quick tears.

"Oh, I do. I'm so glad to see someone. Anyone! Our water isn't coming again. The calves are bawling, and I was going to walk to the firehouse for help."

Quickly, Isaac scrambled to the back and sat primly on a hay bale with his hands clasped jubilantly on his knees. Now she would have to sit beside Sim.

She took Sim's proffered hand, sat down gingerly, and turned to look at him, saying, "You have no idea how glad I am to see you. I'm just desperate. My mam can't go out in this, and I can see the roads are all but impassable."

Sim only nodded, and Isaac thought, Oh, come on now, say something.

"I hope we don't meet a snowplow," Catherine said.

"These horses should be okay. They're used to just about anything."

Isaac pumped the air with his fist, quickly folding it into his other hand when Catherine turned, saying, "Hey, Isaac! I took your seat."

In the distance, they heard the ominous rattling of chains, the dragon let out of his lair, that abominable snowplow. Sim tightened his grip on the reins; Isaac could tell by the squaring of his shoulders. The humongous yellow vehicle rolled into view, spraying a mountain of white snow to the side, chains squeaking and rattling. Pet and Dan lifted their heads, pricked their ears forward, while Catherine grabbed Sim's arm with one hand, stifling a scream with the other.

Perfect! Just perfect!

Isaac knew these Belgians wouldn't do much, if anything, and sure enough, they plodded on as the monstrous truck rattled by.

"Sorry! I'm so sorry," Catherine said.

Sim grinned down at her, saying, "That's all right, Catherine. I wouldn't mind meeting another one."

Yes!

Up went Isaac's fist, then he brought it down and banged it against his knee, squeezing his eyes shut as he dipped his head.

And they still had to fix the water pump.

Isaac had to walk to school the following morning. The sun was dazzling, the whole world covered in a cold, white blanket of snow. The wind moaned about the house, sending gigantic clouds of whirling snow off rooftops and trees, across hills and onto the roads, especially where there was an embankment to the west.

Scootering was out of the question, that was sure. He tied his lunch box to the old wooden sled. He had greased the runners with the rectangular block of paraffin that Mam used to stiffen her white coverings when she washed and ironed them. This sled used to be Dat's, and it was the undisputed leader of all the sleds at Hickory Grove School.

Teacher Catherine greeted him from her desk with the usual "Good morning, Isaac." He was a bit disappointed, the way she said it sort of quieter than usual, then dropped her head and immediately became quite busy.

Had she seen all that fist-pumping? He certainly hoped not.

Hannah Fisher had only one problem wrong in arithmetic class, and he had 100%, which sent Dora Esh into a spasm of sniffing and carrying on. She even raised her hand and asked if it was wrong if Isaac had boxes instead of cartons for a story problem, trying to make him lose his 100%. Then when Teacher Catherine said it was all right, that the problem had both boxes and cartons in it, she looked as if she was going to start bawling, blinking her eyes like that and getting all red in the face.

Someone should straighten these girls out.

All day, Teacher Catherine acted strangely. Even at recess while sledding, she seemed a bit stiff, her movements calculated, almost self-conscious. He caught her watching him do his English, and when he looked up, she quickly looked away.

That was odd.

But, he supposed, you couldn't get away from the fact that no matter how much he admired his teacher, she was a girl, and they all had a tendency to be strange at times.

You just couldn't figure them out.

Take last evening while they were fixing the pump at Speichers. Sim had soon become aware of the problem, but they had to pull the water pump. Catherine had helped gamely. She watched as Sim tightened something, primed it, stopped and started it, then lowered it and told them to open a spigot somewhere and let it run for awhile until the water ran clear.

She hadn't invited them in.

Just stood out there by the old windmill and talked to Sim. Isaac was freezing. He was hungry. Why couldn't they go inside and have a cupcake? They weren't laughing or having fun at all. They just talked boring stuff about hospitals and her dat and *all mosa*. (alms) He thought Catherine was sort of crying at one point, but he got cold and climbed on the bobsled and covered himself up real good with the buggy blanket.

Once, he peeped out over, and they were still standing there, only closer yet, and Sim's head was going to fall off his shoulders if he leaned forward any more than that.

You couldn't date a girl without laughing, ever. Isaac's toes were so cold he stuck them under the hay bale and got steadily angrier. Just when he thought he was going to die of cold and starvation, alone on that bobsled, he heard footsteps, a "Good-night!" and they were off.

He told Sim what he thought, too, and Sim called him "little buddy" and put an arm around his shoulder. Sim said he was sorry it took so long, then burst into some hymn about how great is our God.

Isaac didn't appreciate being called little buddy, either. He was as tall as the eighth-graders, and told Sim so. Then Sim got all emotional about that, so Isaac was thoroughly turned off by the time he got into the warm kitchen.

They ate by the light of the kerosene light: beef stew kept warm in the gas oven, thick with soft buttery dumplings, piles of sweet applesauce, and slice after slice of homemade bread and church peanut butter. Joes had church at their place, and his sister Naomi made a whole batch of the spread. She told Mam that was way too much, that next time she was going to use only two jars of marshmallow cream. Well, at least they had church peanut butter, which was by far the best thing ever.

They practiced for the Christmas program in the afternoon at school. Isaac sincerely hoped Abraham Lincoln liked his wife better than he liked Ruthie.

She acted so dumb. She was supposed to look at him when she spoke her lines, but she looked at his right suspender. He checked it to make sure there was nothing wrong with it, like a stink bug sitting on it, but it just looked like his left suspender, unless the stink bug had flown off. They could fly. He told Calvin that once, and he said, yeah, every time a stink bug flew around the propane gas lamp his mam would scream and point and back away, saying it would put a hole in the mantle and burn the house down. Isaac really laughed about that.

The practicing went terribly wrong.

He pitied Teacher Catherine. She kept a brave face, but no one spoke loud enough, they all droned their lines in a sort of monotone and Ruthie said "Heerod" for King Herod, then got all red-faced and muttery when Teacher Catherine corrected her.

It was a good thing they still had over three weeks to practice.

When Isaac yelled "Bye, Teacher!" at the end of the day, she was staring absent-mindedly out the window at the flying snow and didn't hear him.

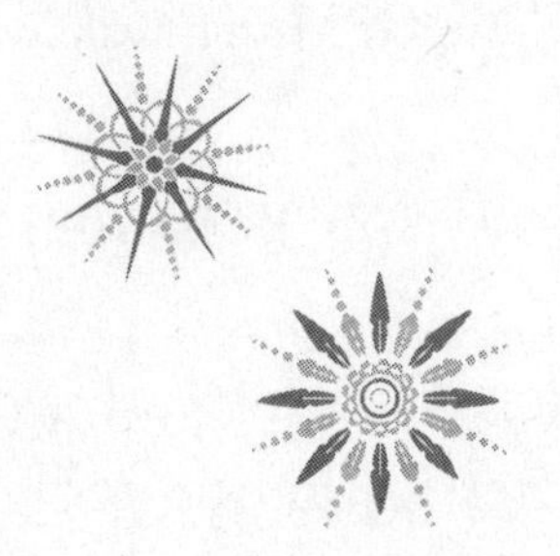

Chapter Four

THE SUN SHONE, THE WINDS MELLOWED AND the days turned into fine winter weather, the kind that are blissful for sledding.

Recess was never long enough. Teacher Catherine was kind enough to allow an extra 30 minutes on Friday, but told them the Christmas program was more important than sledding, and they still had a long way to go.

Isaac knew that was true. They didn't talk plainly. Most of the students spoke in resounding tones, but their words jammed together until no one could understand very well what the poem was about.

How to tell them to speak clearly without being insulting? Teacher Catherine took to pacing the floor, adjusting the shoulders of her cape unnecessarily, sliding her sleeves above the elbow and gripping one forearm with the other until her knuckles turned white.

When it was Isaac's turn to recite his 14-verse poem, he faced the classroom squarely, lifted his chin and spoke in the best way he could possibly muster.

It's Christmas tonight.
The hills are alight,
With the wonderful star of God's love.

On and on he intoned the words of Jesus' birth. They were well-spoken, perfect and he knew it. Teacher Catherine nodded her head, praised him for his clear speech and asked the rest of the class to follow his example. He knew his face was turning a hateful shade of pink as he made his way back to his desk, so he watched the glossy floor tiles closely, wishing his bangs were longer still. Calvin grinned openly and raised his eyebrows.

They practiced three songs, which went well, especially "Joy to the World," which started on a high note. Everyone knew most of the words, and the voices rollicked along together in holiday harmony, which really perked up Teacher Catherine's mood.

After that, little first-grader Eli said his poem in a voice only a decibel above a whisper, his voice shaking with nervous tension. Isaac knew the teacher would not be able to correct him, Eli being so close to tears.

Christmas programs were tough. You had to walk that delicate balance of praise and admonishment, nurturing and controlling.

Ruthie Allgyer sniffed, ducked her head and searched for the ever-present plastic packet of Kleenexes.

Isaac looked out the window and observed Elam King hauling manure with his mules, their large heads wagging in unison, their ears flapping back and forth in their ungainly fashion, as if they were much too big for their heads. He shouldn't be hauling manure. The snow was too deep, adding to the heavy load on the spreader.

Dat said it was hard for the horses to keep their footing, so instead they'd get ready to butcher the five hogs in the shed next week. Isaac knew he'd be cleaning the kettles, and sharpening knives and saw blades in anticipation of the butchering.

When he looked back to the front of the classroom, he was shocked to see Ruthie Allgyer standing in complete misery, her face red with exertion, her mouth working, devoid of any sound at all.

Isaac couldn't watch.

He heard a sob, and a wave of heat washed over him. His heart lurched, feeling her embarrassment keenly. His fingers trace a carved R on his desktop, as he heard Teacher Catherine say kindly, "Ruthie, you may go back to your seat."

Ruthie bent her head, held the white Kleenex to her face and pushed her feet along the floor in humiliation. She slid wretchedly into her desk, folded her arms on the top and buried her face into them as she cried softly.

Isaac couldn't believe it.

Ruthie Allgyer, of all people!

She stuttered?

When had that all started? She hadn't stuttered last year. He remembered everyone saying their poems, Ruthie among them.

Hannah Fisher was next, so she started in her singsong roar. She spoke so loudly you couldn't even hear the words, then plucked the shoulders of her dress in the most self-assured manner it set Isaac's teeth on edge. Well, that Hannah could be set back a notch, in his opinion. Dat said pride went before a fall, so she better watch it.

Isaac pitied Ruthie so badly. He would be extra kind to her, maybe even say something encouraging at recess if he got a chance.

Maybe she dreaded the Christmas program because she had a stuttering problem that was only visible if she had to speak to a crowd. Maybe that was why she looked so anxious and picked her face.

The students colored bells, candy canes and candles, and hung up letters that said, "Merry Christmas." They made paper chains with red and green construction paper and hung them from the four corners of the ceiling to the middle.

There was no Christmas tree and no Santa Claus anywhere. The Amish *ordnung* did not permit either one. Santa Claus was a myth, and Christmas trees were too fancy or worldly and were frowned upon.

The Amish believed in gift-giving because the wise men brought gifts to the Baby Jesus, and God gave the greatest gift of all when he gave the world his son. But presenting gifts was to be done *in maus und maz-ich-keit* (with common sense) and not to follow the ways of the world with very large gifts no one could afford.

That, too, varied in each household. Isaac's parents were conservative with their gifts, giving one package to each child, usually something useful.

Calvin got five or six packages, things Dat

would deem frivolous. Calvin had a Game Boy with a pile of expensive games, something Isaac could only dream about.

It wasn't that he wouldn't have enjoyed having one, it was just the way of it. When you knew something was truly off limits, there was no getting around it. You just read the *Outdoor Life*, ate your whoopie pie and drank milk in the evening and didn't even think about a Game Boy.

Sometimes he felt left out, just a bit, when Calvin and Michael, the other eighth-grade boy, would discuss the games or bring one to school to trade with each other. But not for long. Calvin would always return to Isaac, saying he'd never have a sled that would beat Isaac's old wooden Lightning Flyer, and then Isaac's whole world righted itself.

At recess, Isaac was waiting in line to fill his drinking cup at the water hydrant when Ruthie stepped behind him. Turning around, Isaac faced her squarely and said, "Ruthie, you don't have to be ashamed. Did you know a whole pile of people struggle with not being able to talk in front of a crowd?"

At first anger flashed in her big brown eyes, but then she bobbed her head in acknowledgment. Isaac had never noticed she had freckles on her dark skin.

"Seriously, Ruthie, you can do it. Just don't get so nervous."

"I'm not nervous."

"What is it then?"

Ruthie shrugged her shoulders.

"Did you talk to your mam?"

"Of course not."

"Maybe she could help you."

"I'd never tell my mam."

"Why?"

A shrug of the shoulders and Ruthie fled. So much for that. He knew he could help her. He had read about that somewhere. He'd ask Sim, too.

On Saturday, they attended a Christmas horse sale in New Holland. Isaac had barely been allowed to go along, not having swept the loose hay in the forebay the way Dat wanted him to. He had been sternly lectured, the big calloused hand coming down on his shoulder afterward, saying there was no room in the buggy tomorrow morning for boys who didn't listen.

Isaac had blinked tears of humiliation and pushed the stiff bristled broom like a person possessed, bending his back low with the effort.

He hated displeasing Dat. It was just that he had practiced shooting at tin cans with his BB gun, hitting them dead center in the end, after the winter light had faded to gray. Then supper was ready, and he forgot about the forebay.

That, and Sim had really made him mad, mooning around the barn with his eyes rolling around in his head like a coon hound. He couldn't even focus them right, cutting his finger with his pocketknife when he opened the twine on the bales of straw. Then Sim blamed Isaac for taking too long watering the pigs.

"Do you have any idea how much water five pigs can drink?" Isaac had shouted, sending a good-sized snowball flying in Sim's direction.

When Sim turned around and started after him, Isaac clapped his straw hat on his head and took off, slipping and sliding, sheer terror lending acceleration to his booted feet. Sim grabbed his coat collar, hauled him back, rolled him in the snow and washed his face thoroughly, the snow melting in icy rivulets down his green shirt collar.

They sat together then. Isaac wiped his face with his coat sleeve and told Sim he was lucky he wasn't wearing his glasses, or he'd end up paying for a new pair. Sim laughed and asked how his day at school went.

"Catherine looked extra pretty, thank you very much," Isaac answered, narrowing his eyes.

"I didn't ask about her."

"You did. You don't care about my day one bit. Catherine is also having a hard time with this Christmas program. I'm the only one who says his poem right."

"I bet."

"I'm serious."

Sim smiled.

"But that poor Ruthie. You know, Levi Allgyer's Ruthie. She's in my grade, and she couldn't say her poem. Her face was so red, Sim. It was painful to watch. The words just wouldn't come out."

"What did Catherine do?"

"She was so kind. She just asked Ruthie to go to her seat, and I saw them talking at recess."

Then Sim's eyes got all stupid again, his mouth lopsided and wobbly, and he didn't hear Isaac when he asked if it was true that you could help someone with a stuttering problem.

"Right, you can?" Isaac asked louder.

"Yeah."

But Isaac knew Sim hadn't heard him, so on the way to the horse sale, Isaac scooted forward from the back seat, stuck his head between Dat's and Sim's shoulders and pursued the subject of stuttering once again.

They had stopped at a red light on Route 23 in the town of New Holland. There was traffic everywhere, boxing them in, and Sam the driving horse was a bit too energetic to hold completely still, waiting for that light to change. He hopped up and down on his front feet, so Dat had to hold a steady rein and didn't answer until the light turned green and they could surge forward with the traffic.

Dat reached down and turned the right-turn signal on after they had moved swiftly for about a block before he answered. "You'd think one of Levi's daughters wouldn't have that problem. He's quite a talker."

"I read somewhere that you can help people who stutter. You get them to talk very slowly. Or something like that." Isaac said this a bit hesitantly, afraid Sim would laugh, but he didn't, just nodding his head in agreement.

Horse sales were magical. The flat, long, white buildings were surrounded by vehicles, trailers and black carriages belonging to the Mennonites who drive buggies, the Joe Wengers, as they were known by the Amish. They lived side by side in unity, but the Joe Wengers were an entirely different sect of plain people. The Amish buggies were gray with black wheels; that's how you told them apart.

White fences divided the pens of horses and ponies. Motors hummed, people talked and the auctioneer could be heard from the vast sea of concrete that was the parking lot. The horses milled about, whinnying, tossing their heads.

Dat gave Isaac a five-dollar bill for his lunch. It wasn't enough, but Isaac was ashamed to tell Dat, so he asked Sim for more.

Sim raised his eyebrows. "You can buy a hot dog with five dollars."

"Not French fries and Mountain Dew."

Sim shook his head but extracted his wallet and handed him five one-dollar bills. "You can't go to a horse sale without buying candy and chewing gum."

Isaac couldn't believe it. Another five dollars! At the most he had planned on another dollar, maybe two.

"Hey, thanks, Sim." He ran off before Sim changed his mind.

He'd drink all the Mountain Dew he wanted. That was the best drink anyone had ever invented. He could drink a gallon and never tire of it. Mam said it was not good for little boys, rotting their teeth and supplying too much sugar and caffeine, but Isaac couldn't see the difference in drinking a few cans of the delicious soda, or sitting around at sister's day drinking pot after pot of coffee. They were like camels at a watering trough, never getting enough, those sisters.

Isaac sized up the dollar bill, turning George Washington's head the same way it was imprinted on the Pepsi machine. He held his breath as it gobbled the dollar, then whirred softly, and with a clattering sound his green and red can of Mountain Dew rolled into the little tray.

Expertly, he popped the top, and turned to see Catherine Speicher watching him.

Chapter Five

It was unsettling, sort of.

Teachers were teachers in the classroom, dressed a certain way, always professional, sort of untouchable, set apart.

Here she was, standing in the bright December sun, her hair as light as an angel's, wearing a black coat fancier than the one she wore to school, with a red scarf thrown loosely over one shoulder.

Isaac held his Mountain Dew, then returned her smile, and said, "Hey, Teacher!"

She looked at him a moment longer, and for one mortifying second, he thought she was going to hug him. "Isaac! It's good to see you!"

"Yeah. You, too. You buying a horse?"

She laughed, adjusting her scarf.

"Actually, I am helping at the tack shop today. My friend Liz helps her dat when they're busy before Christmas."

"That's nice."

She hesitated for only a second, then asked, "Are you here by yourself?"

"No, I came with Dat and Sim."

Was it his imagination, or did her face change color only a bit? Perhaps it was the red scarf that gave her cheeks that glow.

He'd have to find Sim, which he accomplished in short order, weaving his way in and out of the crowd, searching the seating area where you could pretty much find someone easily, the seats stacked up the side of the room like bleachers at English peoples' stadiums.

There he was.

Isaac plopped himself in the seat beside Sim, and said, "Catherine Speicher is helping her friend Liz at the tack stand."

That got his attention.

He looked very nice, with that narrow-brimmed straw hat he wore, turned down in the front and back with a piece of rawhide knotted around the crown instead of the black band that belonged there traditionally. A lot of the youth didn't wear hats, but Sim was older, a member of the church, and Dat's ways were deeply ingrained and respected.

Maybe, though, Catherine wouldn't match. For one instant, this flashed through Isaac's head. She was definitely not quite like Sim, and maybe Sim was right that he didn't stand a chance.

No, you just couldn't think along those lines. God wasn't like that. You just took a chance, went ahead and asked the question to see what happened.

"So, are you going to ask her for a date?" he asked, after a long swallow of the sweet soda.

"No, Isaac."

"Why not?"

"Because."

"That's no answer."

"Go away."

"Oh, come on, Sim. You big 'fraidy cat. Just go down to the tack stand and act like you need a new halter, and when she hands it to you, say, 'Could I come see you on Saturday evening at 8:00?'"

"It's not that easy!" Sim hissed. "And don't talk so loud."

Isaac found Tyler, the neighbor boy, who was horse-and-buggy Mennonite. He wore jeans and a thick coat with a zipper and a narrow-brimmed gray hat. Tyler talked with a different accent, although it was the same Pennsylvania Dutch that Isaac spoke.

They clambered up on the wooden fences, perched there and watched the horses milling about. Tyler said the horse dealers drugged the ponies so everyone thought they were safe, and once the drugs wore off, some of them were wild and vicious. Isaac said Dat never bought ponies at an auction, and Tyler said that was smart.

They got to the food stand early, and bought cheeseburgers and French fries and more Mountain Dew. They tapped the glass ketchup bottle hard and a whole glug of it clumped on to their fries, but that was fine with them. They loved ketchup.

They talked about school and Christmas and sleds. Someone stopped at their table, and Isaac looked up to find Catherine Speicher with a tray of food.

"May I sit with you? The tables are all full."

"Sure."

Isaac slid over immediately, and she sat beside him.

"I'm starved; no breakfast."

She ate hungrily, saying nothing. Tyler's father came to get him, so that side of the table was empty, until Sim came in with his lunch and slid in opposite them.

Catherine stopped eating, then, and got all flustered and acted so dumb Isaac could not believe it.

Sim took off his hat and asked if they'd prayed. Catherine shook her head. They bowed their heads for a short while, then Sim began eating his ham hoagie. He had coffee, too, which seemed awfully mature. Isaac was glad, him being so confident and all.

They talked, and Catherine's face turned pink, and then it turned a greenish-white, and sort of leveled off to the usual color as she finished her roast beef sandwich. Isaac sat in the corner and drew down his eyebrows and made "Ask her!" motions with his mouth, which did absolutely no good.

They talked about the snow and school, and who went to which crowd, all having names the way the youth did nowadays. There were Eagles and Pine Cones and Hummingbirds and what not. The wilder youth had their own group; the more conservative ones their own as well. Some of them had rules and were parent-supervised, which turned out well. Sim was with the Eagles, but not the same group as Catherine, since she was so much younger and all.

Oh, she and Sim could talk all right. Endlessly. Same as the night they fixed the water pump.

Well, this was enough. Sim wasn't even close to asking her for a date, so what was the use talking about all this other stuff? Who cared if there was a singing here, or a supper crowd there, or who was marrying who after Christmas?

Just when Isaac was seriously thinking of sliding down beneath the table and crawling out over their feet, Dat came by, looking for him. Catherine blushed again. She said "Hello," very politely, answered Dat's questions respectfully and then let Isaac out of the booth.

Isaac could see the pure elation on Sim's face when Dat said he bought a pair of Belgians, and would Isaac like to ride home in the truck with him?

When Isaac looked back on his way out of the

dining area, Sim was leaning forward with that intent look of his, and if he wasn't careful he'd have to have his back adjusted at the chiropractor's office to put his head back in place.

But Sim just wasn't getting anywhere, that was the whole trouble.

At home, Isaac decided to talk to Mam about the impossibility of the whole situation. It was Saturday afternoon, and she was taking five loaves of whole-wheat bread from the oven. Her gray apron was pinned snugly around her ample waist, covering the front of her dark purple dress. Her covering was large and white, the wide strings pinned together behind her back to keep them from getting in her way as she moved effortlessly from table to stove and back again.

There were four pie crusts cooling on the countertop, so Isaac broke off a tiny piece. Mam yelped and came bustling over, saying, "*Doo net! Doo net.* (Don't) They're for Barbara, for church. Don't touch them. I'm making coconut cream."

"Never chocolate," Isaac muttered.

Like a fluffy, warm comforter, her heavy arm enfolded his shoulders as she steered him to the refrigerator and opened the door, proudly producing a wonderfully high chocolate pie, crowned with an amazing amount of whipped cream and chocolate shavings.

Isaac turned his face to his mother's.

"For us?"

So often, these wonderful concoctions that Mam made on Saturday afternoons were for someone else. Chocolate layer cakes, loaves of bread, creamy vanilla pudding were usually all "for church."

"For you, Isaac! Just for you!" Her words were better than Mountain Dew. What a mother!

"Mam, did you really bake this chocolate pie for me?"

"Yes, for you."

Love looked and tasted exactly like that pie. It was cool and creamy, rich, the chocolate neither too light or too bitter. He ate two wide slices, then asked Mam what she thought of Sim asking Catherine Speicher for a date.

Mam's eyes opened wide, she threw her hands in the air, then folded herself into a kitchen chair and said, "Good lands! You make me weak." She shook her head.

"He likes her. He just doesn't have the nerve to ask her for a date," Isaac said, scraping up the last of the chocolate pudding with his fork.

Mam said there was more to it than that. Dates had to be prayed about and God's leading felt. It always took patience. She wasn't even aware of the fact that they knew each other, and besides, Sim was older, and she thought the teacher a bit fancy. For us, she said.

Isaac told her that had absolutely nothing to do with it, look at him and Calvin. Mam nodded and said maybe that was true, and that Abner Speicher's family was a nice family. It was just that Abner wasn't too good with money, and now he was sick in the hospital. She made that clucking sound.

Isaac told her money has absolutely nothing to do with it either. Did God check out money before he put two people together?

Mam wagged her finger at him and said he better watch it, he was getting too big for his britches. She would talk to Sim about this, he needed to be careful, Catherine was … then she didn't know what to say.

Isaac shrugged into his chore coat, slapped his straw hat on and went to start the chores. Sim was batty as a loon. He was either whistling or looking as if he would burst into tears at the slightest provocation.

Isaac ignored him.

Even when Sim showered, shaved, dressed up and left with his sorrel horse and buggy, he ignored him. He didn't talk to Mam about it again, either.

In the morning he tumbled out of bed and did all his own chores, plus Sim's, when Dat told him Sim was attending church services in another district. Well, that was a fine thing to do. Why would he go off to another church district if Catherine Speicher was in this one? So much for the budding relationship today.

But as these things went, Isaac forgot about Sim, dressed in his Sunday black suit with his white shirt, heavy black felt hat, gloves and boots. Isaac went with Dat and Mam to church at Johns. John was married to his sister Barbara, Bennie's mother.

By the time all the women had been seated on their side, and the men on the other side, and it was finally the boys' turn to file into the warm basement, his toes felt like 10 nuggets of ice. He was cold and sleepy and not in the mood to sit on that hard bench for three hours. Isaac slumped forward and put his chin in the palm of his hand, until he caught Dat's eye. Dat drew his eyebrows down and shook his head slightly, the sign of disapproval.

So Isaac snapped to attention, held his corner of the heavy *Ausbund*, and tried to look attentive and alert. The slow German hymn rose and fell, babies cried, fathers got up to take them to their mothers.

When the minister stood to begin the sermon, Isaac listened to his voice, hearing the usual German verses he heard most Sundays, followed by an explanation in Pennsylvania Dutch. The real German (*hoch Deutsch*) was still read and used in the sermon, but explained in the everyday Pennsylvania Dutch as well, for the children and those who found the German difficult. It was, indeed, an old and precious tradition, to be well-versed in both German and Pennsylvania Dutch. It came easy to Isaac, so he understood and recognized most everything from both sermons.

He fell asleep once, the minister's face swimming in a sea of black-clad men, and he knew nothing for awhile. He was dimly aware of his head drooping to the left. He was so glad to sing the last hymn, then shuffle his way out to the blinding white snow, free at last.

Isaac ate at the last table, after the men and women had already eaten. His stomach was so painfully empty that his head hurt. It was the most cruel thing to eat breakfast so early and dinner so late. He spread a thick slice of homemade bread with soft cheese spread made with white American cheese and milk cooked together, piled on a liberal amount of ham, speared two red beets and a sweet pickle and began to feel instantly better.

Teacher Catherine was pouring coffee at the boys' table, dressed in a purple dress and a white organdy cape and apron. Isaac thought what a golden opportunity Sim was missing. When she poured his coffee, Sim could ask her for a date, very quietly, of course, but he could.

If Sim never got it accomplished, it sure wasn't for lack of his younger brother's great ideas. Or his subtle scouting skills, for that matter.

Chapter Six

Hickory Grove school was a beehive of activity the following Friday. All lessons had been put aside, serious artwork taking up everyone's attention. The classroom must be decorated for Christmas.

They had already accomplished quite a bit, Teacher Catherine said, but they seriously needed to apply themselves, finishing the Christmas poster on the north wall between the two sets of windows. They hung navy blue construction paper for the back drop, which was the upper grade boys' assignment. Elmer's School Glue was used to attach all the pieces.

Michael took charge of the glue, applying it entirely too liberally. It squeezed out when he rubbed his fingers along the edge, so Calvin told him he was using too much, and Michael's face got red and he told Calvin he didn't know everything. That was when Isaac decided to work on the pond. It looked safer.

They leaned over the Ping-Pong table in the middle of the classroom, construction paper scattered everywhere, the tension crackling between them since Michael said that. As soon as Michael got up to get another bottle of glue, Calvin raised his eyebrows, Isaac pointed to the white construction paper and Calvin nodded. He glued the rectangular sheets of construction paper, then whispered to Calvin about the shape of the pond.

"Whatever you think, Professor," Calvin whispered back.

Yes!

Isaac knew he could do the shape of the pond

very well, making it look realistic. After all the construction paper was in place, they'd draw in bushes and trees, stars and a moon, skaters, horses tied and blanketed and a bonfire. It would be a grand poster, one the parents would talk about all Christmas season.

The girls were making bells with cardboard egg boxes. They cut out the little cups that contained the eggs and punched a hole in the top. They covered them with crinkly squares of aluminum foil, strung red and green yarn through them and hung their "bells" from the roller shades by the windows. They were Christmasy looking, Isaac thought, especially with those brilliant red, green and white candy canes in the background.

The white construction paper was designed, cut and attached by Isaac, and then the three boys stood back and admired their efforts.

Teacher Catherine came over and said it was very well done, and that the trees would look great done with black and brown Magic Markers.

"What about snow?" Isaac asked.

Teacher Catherine put one finger to her mouth, tilted her head to the side and considered this.

"There's no snow on the pond," Calvin volunteered.

"Good thinking, Calvin. The snow may have blown off the branches," she said.

Isaac thought snow on the branches was an essential, mostly because the pine trees in the background would look so much better with snow on them, but figured he'd stay quiet. Dat often told him how important it was to give up your own opinion for a better one. It was more influential in the long run to keep your opinion to yourself, if it meant working together in peace and harmony as the end result.

Take barn raisings. Someone had to be the *fore gaya*, the one who ran the whole business. If each worker recognized this, contributed his share of talent, giving and taking, it worked.

One Sunday morning Dat explained the Scripture about the lion laying with the lamb, and he said it meant each of us must lay down our own nature to get along with others. Isaac had mulled that one over for days, and he still didn't get it, really, but figured he didn't have to until he was older.

Teacher Catherine was very pretty today, he thought. Her face shone with a soft light. Her red dress made her look like Christmas, her black apron just slightly lopsided from moving around, bending over desks, always trying to be at two places at one time. Well, the way these lower graders raised their hands was ridiculous. How could she be expected to get anything of her own accomplished?

Then Sarah started crying, rubbing her eyes, mewling like a lost kitten, her lips pouting, as she haltingly told Teacher Catherine that her puppy was supposed to be gray and it looked brown and wasn't nice.

What a *brutz-bupp*! (Crybaby)

Sarah should have used a gray color instead of a brown one. She was in third grade and old enough to know better. Isaac thought Teacher

Catherine should straighten her out, but no, her ever-loving kindness and patience was unfurled like a pure white flag, an example for the impatient ones like Isaac. Putting a hand on Sarah's shoulder, she bent low, assuring Sarah that if she didn't like the color of her puppy, she could start over with a new copy. Sarah wiped her eyes, sniffed, then marched proudly to the teacher's desk for another copy, one woolen black sock falling sloppily over her Skechers. Third graders were an annoyance, no question. But if you went to a one-room Amish school, you just had to put up with them, that was the way of it.

So now. Night sky and pond in place. This was going to be awesome!

"Boys," Teacher Catherine announced. "The girls will soon be finished with their bells, so they may help you with the freehand drawing of figures, horses, whatever. Isaac?"

Before he could stop himself, his arm shot up. "Well, we can't have just anyone helping, can we?"

Then he was subject to the most awful glare of

disapproval. It shot from her blue eyes, a laser of reproach. Not one word was necessary.

Isaac felt his face fire up to about 500 degrees. He wished he could turn into an ant and disappear beneath the baseboard.

He should have stayed quiet.

But these girls and their cutesy-pie drawings of flowers and butterflies and birds and stuff. How could they ever be expected to come up with anything decent? This poster was serious material.

Isaac cringed when Ruthie hung the last cluster of bells on the window shade and went to the cupboard for art paper. He had to admit, though, they had done a real good job on those handmade bells.

"Put your books away for lunch," Teacher Catherine announced. Instantly there was a rustle of paper, heads bent to put things in their desks. "Davey, is it your turn to pass the waste can?"

Davey nodded happily, picked up the tall Rubbermaid waste can and slowly wended his way down the aisle as everyone hurried to throw their crumpled paper, bits of crayon, and colored pencil shavings into it before he moved on.

The wooden desks all had a hole cut on top, to the right, where pupils had kept their inkwells in times past. There were no more antique ink pens, of course, so that hole was perfect for stuffing crumpled waste paper.

Hickory Grove School was an older one, so they still had those desks, but the newer ones were made without the hole. Dan Stoltzfus and his helpers made school desks now, sleek and smoothly finished, the steel parts painted black, all glossy and shiny like the buggies.

Some of the Amish schools got the desks the English schools no longer needed. They were not attached to the floor, the lids opened and you could see your whole cache of books and stuff at once. Nothing fell out of those desks, which was nice, but the teachers complained about them being noisy, saying the tops were propped up too long while bent heads did a lot of whispering behind them.

Dora got the teakettle from the stove top, poured the steaming hot water into the blue plastic dishpan, then carried it to the hydrant beside the porch to add cold water. Why didn't she fill it half-full with cold water first, then add the hot? If she thought, she wouldn't have to carry all that hot water out the door.

You simply couldn't get past it. Girls had very little common sense.

She set the dishpan on a small dry sink, added a squirt of anti-bacterial soap, and washed her hands, drying them with brown paper towels from the dispenser on the wall.

"First row," Teacher Catherine said. Row after row, the scholars filed in an orderly fashion, washing their hands, drying them, grabbing their lunch boxes from the cloakroom and returning to their seats. Teacher Catherine bowed her head, the pupils followed suit and they sang their dinner prayer in a soft melody.

When they finished, the "amen" fading away, most of the pupils made their way to the front of the room, where the propane-gas stove held dozens of foil-wrapped sandwiches, hot dogs, chicken patties, or small casseroles containing the previous evening's leftovers. Tiny Tupperware containers of ketchup were scraped over hot dogs and chicken patties and put on a roll. Juice boxes or containers of milk washed down the good, hot food.

Calvin opened his lunch and produced a ham sandwich loaded with lettuce and tomato. He popped the top of a can of grape juice and grinned at Isaac, who was wolfing down his sandwich made of homemade wheat bread, sweet bologna and mustard. A pint jar of chocolate milk, made with the good creamy milk straight from the bulk tank in the milk house and flavored with Nestle's Quik, accompanied his sandwich. Mam bought the chocolate mix in large yellow cylinders at Centerville Bulk Food Store. Sometimes he wished Mam would buy fancy Tupperware drink containers the way other mothers did, but she said all her children used glass pint jars for their chocolate milk, and she had no intention of stopping now.

There was a gasp from Ruthie, as Daniel and Reuben started to tussle, spilling Daniel's juice all over everything.

Teacher Catherine laid down her sandwich deliberately, her mouth set in a straight line as she got up, grabbed Reuben by the arm and marched him back to his seat. "You know you have to stay in your seat at lunchtime," she said firmly. Isaac didn't know whether Reuben was pinched, or if the reprimand alone was enough, but he bent his head and cried softly.

The classroom became devoid of sound as Daniel was marched to sit in an empty desk, without his juice. Dora helped mop up the sticky mess with paper towels, but it was Teacher Catherine who had to use warm water and soap in a bucket, get down on her knees and wipe it all up properly, while her sandwich got cold.

It served that Reuben right. Daniel, too. Those little second graders couldn't hold still one minute, not even long enough to eat their lunches.

The pupils had to remain seated for 15 minutes, which was the most cruel thing the school board had ever invented. You could easily eat a sandwich in five minutes, drink all your chocolate milk, grab your bag of pretzels and be out the door.

Recess was only 45 minutes, which wasn't long enough at all. Especially now, with all this snow. So they ate in a big hurry, sat together with their feet in the aisle, traded snacks and talked.

Calvin said there was a fire on the other side of Georgetown; the fire engines had made an awful racket. Isaac asked him how he knew already, and Calvin shrugged his shoulders, so Isaac figured one of his brothers who was at the *rumspringa* age had a radio or a cell phone, maybe both.

You just didn't talk about those things in school, those objects being *verboten* (forbidden) the way they were. It was not a good subject to discuss, especially with the more conservative children like Isaac, whose family would never own anything the church frowned on. It was called respect.

Isaac knew Calvin's brothers were not like Sim. They each had had a vehicle for a short time, even. Isaac and Calvin never talked about it, though, which was good. That was a separate world, and to avoid that subject meant they could like each other tremendously. They lived in their own young world of friendship, discussing only matters of importance, like horses and sleds and scooters, and really awesome ideas like making a better scooter, how to fire up a stove with the right kindling and who was the best skate sharpener in Lancaster County.

When the long hand on the clock finally reached the three, they moved fast and efficiently, throwing their lunch boxes on the shelf with one hand, grabbing their coats and hats or beanies with the other, and moving to the front door with long strides that were not really running, but certainly not quite walking, either.

The minute their heads popped out the door, a nanosecond ahead of their feet, yells of pure elation broke out. They dashed to their sleds, grabbed the rope handles and raced out of the schoolyard, around the fence, and up Eli Esh's slope.

Sledding was the only time they were allowed out of the schoolyard. They had to be closely supervised, staying off the road until they were safely in the field, which was free from traffic. But the "big boys" were allowed to go ahead, before Teacher Catherine appeared with the smaller ones.

They had already reached the top of Eli's hill and were on the way down. The paths they had cut to smooth perfection on Monday, now slick from the sun's rays, had frozen and melted and frozen again. It made for glorious sledding.

The sun, the flying bits of snow, the absolute speed, the cold, all filled Isaac's mind. So when the horn sounded, the brakes screeched, the children screamed and screamed without stopping, it took a while until he knew something wasn't right.

In fact, something awful had just occurred.

Chapter Seven

ISAAC WAS OFF HIS LIGHTNING FLYER BEFORE it stopped, left it and began to run.

The vehicle had skidded to a haphazard stop, sideways on the road. A small black figure lay inert on the cold, hard macadam.

A middle-aged couple emerged from the car, the man reaching for his wife's hand. Her gloved hand was held across her mouth, her eyes wide with terror.

Teacher Catherine reached Raymond first. She bent, put out a hand, then looked up as the

English man reached her. He got down on one knee. Isaac was relieved to hear a moan, followed by an ear-piercing scream.

It was Raymond! He was conscious.

Isaac was joined by Calvin and Michael, then Jake and Danny, the fifth-grade boys. Teacher Catherine got up, spoke sternly, loudly, as Raymond's screaming continued.

"Take them all inside. Ruthie. Dora. *Nemmat die kinna ny.*" (Take the children in.)

With one wild look at Raymond, the car and the English man and his wife, they obeyed, herding the sobbing huddle of black-clad children back to the schoolhouse, where they promptly stationed themselves on the bench below the windows, watching.

An approaching car stopped. The man got out, assessed the situation and pulled his cell phone from his coat pocket, as Raymond continued his screams of pain.

The English lady dashed back to the car, returned with a crocheted afghan in red and green, then bent to lay it gently over the child.

Teacher Catherine was on her knees beside Raymond, stroking his hair, talking to him in Pennsylvania Dutch, but nothing helped. Raymond just went on screaming.

Isaac could hardly take it. He felt sick to his stomach, and the white, white world went crooked for an instant. He swallowed and was all right.

Why did the fire company take so long? Surely it shouldn't take the medics that much time.

Teacher Catherine left Raymond only long enough to step over and tell the boys to scooter to Jesse Kauffmans' and tell them to come, fast.

The boys ran, grasped their scooter handles, bent low and pedaled furiously, one leg flung back as far as it would go to build momentum.

Raymond's mam was eating her lunch. Her face turned white, but she remained calm, instructing her older daughter Ella Mae to run to the phone shanty and call her dat, who worked at the welding shop in Gordonville.

"*Bleib yusht do,*" (Just stay here.) she told Ella Mae, then hopped on a scooter and followed the schoolboys.

The medic had arrived. Raymond was sedated and put on a stretcher before his mother got there.

Isaac was relieved, glad Jesse *sei* Anna did not have to witness that horrible screaming.

They opened the back doors of the ambulance and loaded Raymond into it. His mother was taken with the English people who had accidentally hit him.

The police swarmed about, their yellow lights whirling on top of their vehicles, their radios crackling, asking questions, jotting down information.

Teacher Catherine remained calm and effective, answering questions. Her face was white, her blue eyes huge, filled with liquid her pride would not allow to spill over. Isaac admired her so much. He sure had a story for Sim.

They went back to the schoolroom and sat in their desks. No one wanted to continue sledding, work on the poster or practice for the Christmas program.

Teacher Catherine asked each family whether their parents were home, and then dismissed the school at one o'clock. She said as soon as she received any news about Raymond's condition, she'd leave them all a message on their voicemail, so they should be sure to check their messages later in the day.

The children nodded soberly. They wended their way quietly out of the schoolyard. Concerned parents wiped tears, hugged their own little ones and were thankful. To be able to hold their warm, healthy little bodies was something, now, wasn't it?

Edna Beiler went to the phone–hers was in the shop on her husband's metal desk–and called her sister Esther, who often heard her phone. Esther had a bell rigged up to it, which was louder than the high insistent whine of an ordinary telephone.

Esther always got her way, that Amos being the kindhearted soul he was. Edna knew her Paul would never rig up a bell to her phone. He said women didn't need to sit there yakking and gossiping all day, so she set her phone in an aluminum cake pan, which increased the sound quite a bit, deciding if Paul didn't like it he could just get her a bell like Esther had.

Thankfully, Esther answered after about six rings, and they had a breathless conversation about Teacher Catherine not watching those children.

Edna said maybe Catherine had been there, and Raymond didn't listen. You know how first-graders are. Barely off their mothers' laps.

Edna said it was a good thing it happened to Jesse Kauffmans, they could afford a hospital bill better than some, and Esther snorted and said nobody could afford a hospital nowadays, no wonder there were so many benefit auctions and suppers.

Edna promptly told her that Paul said maybe they should stop, too much going on all the time, when we're told to live a quiet and restful life.

What's quiet or restful, going, going, going the way everyone did?

That really irked Esther, so she hung up before Edna finished, leaving Edna staring at the black receiver in disbelief. Not knowing what else to do, she took the tip of her apron and cleaned the dust off the black telephone.

Then she dialed Esther's number again.

That was just wrong. She wasn't one bit mad. She had only voiced an opinion. Not even her own, but her husband's. Oh well, they were both upset, felt helpless in the face of this tragedy. What if poor little Raymond died?

When Esther didn't answer the phone, Edna decided she was just as *dick keppich* (thick headed) as she had always been, left the shop in a huff, then cried in her dishwater.

Voicemails were filled with the news much later that evening.

Raymond was home. His collarbone was broken, and he had a bad brushburn on one thigh where the car had thrown him on the rough macadam, but Eli Esh *sei* Barbara was already at Jesse Kauffmans with burdock leaves and B & W ointment. The collarbone would heal on its own, although he came home wearing a stiff, white neck brace. The doctors at Lancaster General allowed the B & W ointment to be used, although Jesses had to promise to report any infection.

The children returned to school a subdued lot, the accident still embedded in their memory, a thorn of pain along with Raymond's.

Esther and Edna forgave each other on the phone the following morning and got together a Sunshine Box, sending messages to dozens of voicemails. Each family was given a letter of the alphabet, and they were to buy a gift starting with that letter. Then the gifts were placed in the Sunshine Box, so that each day Raymond would open one, starting with the letter A.

Poor Sarah ended up with three poems to recite since Raymond couldn't say his, which greatly upset her. She went home and told her mother she felt like she had too much to do at the

Christmas program. So her mother sent a note along to Catherine asking her to reduce Sarah's load. Teacher Catherine asked everyone if they felt they had too much to say. Isaac volunteered to say another poem, so he was allowed to say the one everyone considered too difficult.

The plays were going much better. The pupils only needed to glance briefly at their copies to get it right. Isaac's version of Abraham Lincoln was perfect, Calvin said, especially after they crafted a top hat out of black construction paper.

Then, the front door broke. Jake went flying out, slammed it back against the brick wall and busted the glass. Teacher Catherine's face got red and she made Jake go sit in his seat.

She wrote a note for the school caretaker but he was down with a herniated disk, his back causing him awful grief. Isaac stepped up to the plate, offering Dat's services, secretly plotting not Dat, but Sim's expertise. He knew Sim could replace that window. He'd watched him plenty of times at home.

Gleefully, he cornered Sim in the forebay when he was leading the Belgians to the water trough that evening.

"Hey, the door—the window in the door—at school broke. Henna Zook broke his back, or something like that, so I told Catherine Dat would fix it. You will though, right? Right, you will?"

Sim looked at Isaac, then said he wasn't going to go there when all the children were there, and Isaac said that was fine, Catherine stayed later in the day, he'd go along.

"Maybe you need to stay home."

"If I do, will you ask her?"

Sim showed up at school the next day with a tape measure, while the children flocked around him wide-eyed, watching every move he made. He went off to the hardware store and returned just after everyone had gone home, with Isaac lingering on the front porch.

Perfect!

While Isaac watched, offering advice, Sim worked to remove the broken glass, and then the frame. Teacher Catherine stayed at her desk, checking papers, and nothing happened. Not one thing.

Sim whistled low under his breath, not even glancing in her direction.

She kept her head bent, her blond hair neatly combed back beneath her white covering.

The sun fell lower in the evening clouds, a red orb of inefficient heat in the winter sky, night-time fast approaching, the cold beginning to flex its muscles as Isaac sat on the cement steps.

"Why don't you go on home, Isaac?" Sim suggested.

"I'm going with you."

"You'll freeze your backside, sitting there."

"Will not."

Finally, Sim tapped one last time and bent to retrieve his tools. Then he stood up, fixed his hat, adjusted his coat collar, opened the door, and walked into the classroom.

Isaac followed, eager to watch the action, his eyes bright pools of curiosity.

"How are you, Catherine?" Sim asked, in his deep, manly voice.

She looked up, smiled and didn't look away. She didn't answer, either. She just looked.

So Isaac scrambled happily up on Calvin's desk and sat there.

"I'm fine," Catherine said, and her voice was not shaky and flustered. It had music in it.

"How's your dat?"

"Much better. I haven't seen him with this much energy ever, I don't think. Did I thank you for picking me up that day? In the sled?"

"I don't remember, I'm sure you did."

She laughed, sort of soft and low, and so did Sim, which made absolutely no sense to Isaac. They hadn't even said anything funny, so why did they laugh?

They talked about the accident, and Catherine said she felt bad, still, that if only she would have been quicker she may have prevented it. Sim told her that was total nonsense, no one could have stopped Raymond if he darted into the path of a car that fast.

Catherine shook her head and her blue eyes turned darker and she looked sad, in a way.

Isaac said to Calvin the next day that he thought his brother Sim might like the teacher. Calvin said lots of guys did, but his mam said Catherine was terrible picky; that's why she was still single.

So Isaac figured everything he'd gained pretty much shifted out of his grasp again, Calvin making that comment and Sim looking so dull these days.

The poster was looking more wonderful each day. Ruthie surprised him most. She drew a girl skating backward, going in a tight circle, her skirt and scarf blowing so realistic and all, that Isaac admitted to Michael he didn't know girls could draw freehand like that.

Hannah drew two horses that looked like camels and were about the same color. Isaac told Teacher Catherine they couldn't have those horses on there, and she said they could not hurt

Hannah's feelings, the horses had to stay. Maybe he could draw blankets on them.

Isaac did, then, and the horses looked like camels with horse blankets, but when he colored them a bright shade of red, it looked Christmasy, decorative and colorful enough. Hannah was insulted anyway, sniffing and parading around like a cat that fell in the water trough, saying the horse blankets ruined her horses, so Isaac told her to cover them up with snow.

That really got her going.

Chapter Eight

TEN DAYS THEY HAD.

Teacher Catherine really cracked down on the procrastinators. There was no putting off what could be done today. Those that did not listen and learn their parts would have to give them to someone else.

That got the ball rolling.

No more copies were allowed. The plays had to be memorized, the parts said at the right time with the proper expression, and loudly enough. Teacher Catherine stood against the wall at the back of the classroom, a formidable figure, her lips set in a grim line of determination. The pupils sat up and took notice. She praised, cajoled, stopped the quiet ones and made them do it over, always goading them on.

The only pupil that seemed hopeless was Ruthie. She desperately wanted to speak. She had a lovely poem, but so far, had been totally unable to finish it. She picked her face, cleared her throat, reached behind her back to pin and re-pin her apron, stalled for time, but nothing worked.

Isaac talked to Mam one evening, the best time of the day to approach her when she had just gotten out of the shower. She smelled of lotion and talcum powder. She wore her homemade, blue flannel bathrobe, buttoned down the front with leftover pants buttons, a *dichly*, that triangular piece of fabric she wore to cover her head at night so that when she woke in the middle of the night, she would have her head covered so she could pray for her family, starting with the first and going all the way to Isaac. Her gray hair was wavy after she washed it, loose and wavy, even when it was bound by the ever-present *dichly*, making her appear more girlish, safer, somehow.

"Mam, what do you think of trying to help someone overcome stuttering?"

Mam looked up from the *Blackboard Bulletin* she was reading.

"Why?"

"You know Ruthie? Lloyd's Ruthie?"

Mam nodded.

"She just can't say her poem this year." He described in vivid detail Ruthie's nervousness, her unwillingness to talk to her mother.

Mam shook her head.

"Well, Isaac, I don't want you to think this is looking down on someone, but Ruthie probably doesn't have much of a home life. Her mother and, well ... she has reason to be nervous."

"So what could we do? Is it true that you can help someone stop stuttering, stammering, whatever you want to call it, by speaking slowly?"

"I've heard of it."

"How could we do it?"

"Why don't you start a support group? Sort of a system where all her friends work with her? Ask Teacher Catherine to help you."

Isaac thought that sounded just wonderful. He pitied Ruthie and told Mam so.

Mam said she was glad Isaac had a soft heart. It spoke well for his character.

Isaac usually fell asleep soon after his head touched his pillow, having to get up at 5:00, the way he did.

Tonight, however, was different. He was thinking.

Ruthie could just give up her poem. But he knew for himself, he would be ashamed to be without that solo piece of poetry, everyone expecting it the way they did.

She was about as decent as any girl could be. For one thing, she could draw stuff other than hearts and flowers. She had drawn most of the figures skating on the pond, some of them looking real. And she liked dogs. She had an English Setter of her own named Shelby. That was sort of cool. Shelby. It had a nice ring to it.

He also liked the way her freckles were spattered across her nose, sort of like God put sprinkles on the icing of a cupcake. If he had to pick any girl as his wife, it would have to be Ruthie. He didn't know when he'd heard her sniff last. Or blow her nose.

The next day at first recess, Isaac approached her, after talking to Calvin and Michael.

"How would you like to be helped with your problem of stammering?" he blurted.

"You mean stuttering?" Ruthie asked. Her eyes were watchful.

"Yeah."

"Who would help me? Who would even know how?"

"Me. Me and Calvin and Michael and Hannah and Dora."

"You would?" She sounded surprised and a little pleased.

"Sure."

"When?"

"Every lunch hour, 'til the program."

"Give up sledding?" She asked, considering.

"Mm-hm."

"Ar-aright." Ruthie's eyes shone.

So that was how it started. They called themselves the SOS group. Support Our Stutterer.

Ruthie giggled, twisting her apron. Isaac began by having her read long sentences from a book, anything, as long as she spoke. She could speak perfectly as long as she read from a book, but when she was placed on the stage in front of the blackboard, she could not face anyone and speak a word without stumbling horribly.

When she felt the constriction in her throat begin, they asked her to stop. At first, she was close to tears. She grabbed a corner of her black apron and twisted it, then released it, clearing her throat, blinking her eyes, doing anything she possibly could to avoid eye contact or holding still.

Isaac took charge. Barking instructions, pacing, his voice carrying well, he asked her to look at him. If she wasn't comfortable looking at him, she could look at Hannah.

She shook her head.

So Isaac met her eyes, told her to watch his face, and repeat this sentence.

She got nowhere, her mouth twisting, her throat swelling with the effort of making just one coherent sound. After that, they stopped.

"Okay, Ruthie, let's start by saying sentences while you are sitting with us."

Patiently, they started over. If she read from a book, she was fine, but when she faced anyone, the words stayed in her throat as if someone had closed a gate.

It was time for the bell.

Isaac's shoulders slumped. Michael walked wearily to his desk, Calvin rolled his eyes in Isaac's direction and even Hannah lost a bit of her swagger. They could not accomplish this in nine days. It was hopeless.

Isaac hung around the schoolyard until the last pupils had pushed their way home on their scooters, then returned and entered the classroom.

Catherine was surprised to see him.

"Yes, Isaac?"

"Sorry to bother you, but is there nothing we can do for Ruthie? Do you know of anyone who has overcome this problem? Any books we can read?"

Catherine said nothing, just looked at Isaac without seeing him. Finally she sighed.

"Isaac, can I trust you to keep this bit of information to yourself?"

He nodded.

"Ruthie has a sad life now that her mother is … well, she's in the hospital for … help. She has problems with her thinking. They just found out a few weeks ago that she may have either a tumor on her brain or Alzheimer's."

"What's that?"

"It's when your brain is diseased, in a way, and you no longer function normally."

"Oh."

"I think Ruthie is very afraid. She's trying to go about her life as if nothing is wrong, hoping none of her classmates find out. She carries a deep sense of shame. Her mother has always been ... an excitable woman, to put it mildly, and those children have suffered seriously, in ways you can't imagine. So ... perhaps, Isaac, you could reach her? Maybe if she found out ...."

Catherine's voice drifted off.

"You mean if I told her that I know about her mother and tell her it's all right, stuff like that happens to people all the time, she'd loosen up?"

Catherine nodded.

Isaac pushed himself home, flinging his leg energetically, happy with this bit of information. Teacher Catherine was the best, most beautiful, sweetest person he had ever met. She treated him as her best buddy, letting him in on that secret, doing it in a way that didn't make Ruthie's mother appear mean, just pitiful. Now he believed Ruthie might be able to overcome her crippling stutter, if he did this right.

At home, he grabbed two chocolate chip cookies and ran out the door to find Sim. It was very important that Sim knew about this, especially about Catherine being so wise and pretty, and if he didn't get around to asking her for a date soon, it would be forever too late, the opportunity evaporated like mist from the pond. It was time Sim straightened himself up.

He found Sim loading manure in the heifer barn. The acrid odor met his nostrils before he saw Sim, but he was used to the raw stench of fresh manure, so he climbed the gate and walked over to him.

Hatless, his everyday shirt sleeves rolled up above the elbow and his shoulders bulging beneath the seams of his shirt, Sim was forking great quantities of the sodden stuff with each forkful. He stopped, ran the back of his hand along his forehead, stuck his pitchfork into the remaining manure and smiled at Isaac. "What's up?"

"Hey, you know Lloyd's Ruthie? The girl that

stutters? She can't talk one tiny bit. And you know what?" He related the entire afternoon's visit with his teacher, watching Sim's face, emphasizing Catherine's part.

Sim didn't show any emotion, just scratched a forearm and looked out the door at the snowy landscape.

"And, you know, Sim, if you don't make yourself do it, she's not going to wait around much longer. You need to ask her for a date. Get going once!"

Isaac was surprised at Sim's reaction. Sim looked as if he was going to cry. When he spoke, it was quietly, seriously, almost like a preacher in church.

"All right, little brother. I hear you. And I wish I could tell you okay, I'll ask her. At your age I probably would have. A schoolboy hasn't seen much of life, of love or loss. It's not as simple as you think. And, Isaac, a lot of children your age would not talk the way you do. You're too smart. You see, God comes first. If I pray to him first, ask him for his blessing in my life, then maybe, just maybe, someday, he will allow me to have her. But I have to wait. Wait on his answer."

Isaac snorted loudly, scaring the heifers in the corner watching the pair of Belgians hitched to the manure spreader with frightened eyes.

"Well, and just how does God go about speaking to you? You a prophet, or what? Catherine likes you. You're too dumb to see it."

With that, Isaac climbed back over the fence, popping the last of the chocolate chip cookies into his mouth, and let Sim finish cleaning the heifer barn by himself. If he got out of there fast enough, Sim might not remember the chicken house needed to be cleaned.

Just his luck, he ran into Dat.

"Hi, Isaac! Home from school so soon? How was your day?"

"School."

"That's not much of an answer," Dat said, smiling broadly.

"Same thing. It was just school."

"Christmas program ready yet?"

"Yup."

"Good! I'm looking forward to it."

Isaac smiled at Dat and was rewarded by the warm kindness in his eyes, the same as always.

Dat was like a rock-solid house you could go into and never be afraid of anything or anyone. He was always the same, sometimes busier than others, more preoccupied, but never angry or hateful or rude.

Now he looked at Isaac with a shrewd expression.

"So, do you think a boy like you should be getting a pony spring wagon if he forgets to scrape the chicken house?"

He looked up sharply and found Dat's smile.

"How would you like to drive Ginger to school every day?"

A new spring wagon for ponies! It was hard to grasp.

"You better get busy, Isaac."

Dat reached out, lifted Isaac's torn straw hat and plopped it back down, a gesture of affection.

While Isaac cleaned and scraped, shooing chickens away, he kept repeating, "Wow! Wow!"

Chapter Nine

Isaac fairly flew to school, the thought of the new spring wagon goading him on, his energy buzzing and humming.

The sky looked dark and heavy enough to fall right down on his head. Big piles of iron-gray clouds were flattening themselves into the fishbone shape Mam always spoke of. She said if gray clouds looked like a fish skeleton, gray and flat and straight, there was a wet air from the east, and a rain or snowstorm was approaching.

Dat clucked over the morning paper. "There's another big one coming."

"*Ach, du lieva*!" (Oh, my goodness.) Mam set down her cup of coffee, broke another glazed doughnut in half and took a generous bite, hungrily. And she just had breakfast. "You mean we'll have two storms before Christmas?"

"I would say so. Whatever you do, Isaac, if it gets to *rissling* (ice coming down), wait at school until someone comes to get you. Your scooter isn't safe on the road in those conditions."

Dat was very serious, so Isaac sat up and listened.

At school, he told Calvin about the approaching storm, Calvin nodding and saying already there was a winter storm watch for Lancaster, Berks and Dauphin Counties.

It was dark in the schoolhouse. Teacher Catherine got a lighter out of her desk and lit the propane gas lamp, its warm glow and soft hissing sound wrapping the pupils in homey, familiar light.

It was the only light they were used to at home. A propane tank was set in a pretty oak cabinet, sometimes painted black or off-white or red, depending on the housewife's preference, with a long pipe attached to the head where two mantles were tied. When a tiny flame was held to the mantles, a bright light burst forth, illuminating a whole room easily. It was the best alternative to electricity.

Mam said years ago they didn't have propane lamps. They used naptha gas in a lamp hung from the ceiling. They were right dangerous, in her opinion, but back then you never thought about it. You could burn kerosene in the same lamp, except you had to heat the head with a torch, or use the little cup that was provided for a shot of lighter fluid, ignite it, and then a small, steadily burning blue flame heated the mantles until you could turn the lamp on, which was even more dangerous and time-consuming. So they had come a long way.

Dat shook his head about the fast moving solar and battery operations that were creeping into homes nowadays. Some of the more liberal households no longer used propane lamps, but a 12-volt battery in the oak cabinet attached to a bulb on a real electric lamp that was converted to battery use.

You had to wonder where it would all end, Dat said, stroking his beard and looking very wise. It was important to keep the old traditions, he said. They meant a lot.

Sim said change would come, though, it always had. Look at the milking machines and bulk tanks. Propane gas stoves and refrigerators. Some change was good. Dat agreed, but admonished Sim to be *trick-havich* (hold back) and it would never spite him, reaping the benefits in later years.

As Isaac settled into his desk, he shivered. Normally, the classroom was warm, but the farthest corners were cold this morning. He gazed out the window as Teacher Catherine read the Bible, waiting for those first icy snowflakes to ping against the east side of the schoolhouse. He glanced at Ruthie, appalled to find her blinking, her eyes bright with unshed tears. As he watched, her brown eyes overflowed, the tears leaving wet streaks through her freckles.

He looked away.

When he returned from singing class, he got out his arithmetic book as usual. Now he inserted a piece of paper, and wrote,

> *Ruthie, it's O.K. Teacher Catherine*
> *says it is. I know about your mam.*
> *I feel sorry for her. Hang in there.*
> *You're strong.*
>
> *We're all here for you.*

Isaac knew it was against the rules to pass notes, but when he exchanged his arithmetic paper with her, he put the note inside, then watched steadily out the opposite window while she read it.

That day was a turning point.

It was as if Ruthie had been slipping, unable to gain a foothold. Now, a shaky attempt had paid off. She had found the strength to shake the crippling defeat in her young life.

At the recess SOS group, she repeated sentences, stuttering, straining, sometimes having to be completely quiet. But she spoke.

Then the snowstorm came at suppertime, all right.

It started like granules of salt, so fine and hard, piling into every crack and crevice it could find. It sifted along the cow stable's windowsills, a place Isaac could not remember ever finding snow.

The hen's water froze. They pecked holes into the ice and drank anyway. Dat said to feed the pigs and hens plenty; they'd need extra to keep themselves warm. Isaac and Sim put straw bales around the pigpen, wrapped sheets of insulation, that pink, itchy, fiberglass stuff, around the water hydrants and put a heater in the milk house.

Their Barbara came down with bronchitis, and needed Mam to send over Numotizine.

"What a night!" Mam fumed and fussed. No driver wanted to go out in this weather. She'd be ashamed to call one.

Sim said he'd make the five-mile drive. He had a heater in his buggy. When Isaac offered his company for the ride, Sim grinned and nodded.

Mam put a glob of that vile salve from her own blue and white container in a glass jar. It was an old, old remedy, containing something so awful smelling you could hardly stand to watch Mam put it in a jar, let alone having it applied to your chest with a steaming hot rag slapped on top. It was enough to suffocate a person, having to sleep with that stench, but Mam showed no mercy with her administration of Numotizine. She stated flatly that it had saved her hundreds of dollars in doctor bills, spared her children from antibiotics, and why wouldn't you use these old home remedies from the past?

So in the cold and dark, the snow zooming in through the opened window, Sim and Isaac started out.

With a horse like Sim's you had to keep the window latched to the ceiling for awhile, allowing the cold and snow its entry. There was no other way to do it. For one thing, the small rectangular holes cut in the window frame to allow the leather reins to pass through, were actually too small to handle a spirited horse. Horses always needed a firm hand starting out, and Saddlebred Fred was no exception, the way he hopped around. He shied, he ran way out around the driveway, making a large circle in the alfalfa field, and then dashed down the road as if a ghost was after him.

The steel-rimmed buggy wheels lost traction, swaying and zig-zagging across the quickly disappearing road, as Sim strained to control Fred. Isaac wrapped himself tightly into the plush buggy robe, and hoped the snow plows would hold off until they got home. The way Fred was acting, they'd end up in Philadelphia if they met one.

Sim didn't talk, so Isaac said nothing either. Then, sure enough, the twirling yellow light of a snowplow showed through the gloom, bearing down on them.

"Yikes!" Isaac wasn't planning on saying that; it just slipped out of its own accord.

"Hang on!" Sim shouted.

Isaac couldn't do that, as the buggy went straight down a steep bank. Grimly, he bit down on his lower lip, slid off the seat and socked into the corner of the buggy. Sim was standing up, leaning way back, his gloved hands working the reins, Fred galloping across someone's field out of control.

The buggy swayed and lurched, Isaac cowering in the corner, his eyes squeezed shut, waiting for the moment the buggy would fly into a thousand pieces, his body exploding out of it into the wild black night. It didn't happen. They just slowed down. Fred stopped his headlong gallop.

They made it safely to Barbara's house, who looked as if she needed a hospital more than she needed this Numotizine. She was on the couch, her breathing raspy, her cough sounding like a piece of wood falling down the stairs.

The house was a royal mess. As usual, Bennie wasn't behaving, sitting on the table spreading Ritz crackers with peanut butter. He had everything all over his pants, the table top and his sister Lydia. When Isaac told him to put the peanut butter away, he lifted his face and howled. John came rushing over carrying the baby, who set up her own high-pitched yell, her bottle of apple juice suddenly disappearing as her dat rushed to the rescue.

John glared at Isaac, got a wet cloth and told Bennie to clean up the peanut butter, which was the same as asking a pig to clean up his pen. Isaac sat on the recliner by the stove, disliking Bennie.

He was glad to leave with Sim.

These things, of course, were not talked about. He couldn't tell Sim how much he couldn't stand that Bennie. Sim would say it was a sin, which Isaac knew, but sometimes you could hardly help it.

Sim chuckled to Isaac, saying now that was marriage, and didn't that take the fairy story out of it? This was the real thing.

Isaac hoped fervently Bennie would get a licking from his dad, although he couldn't see that happening.

"Bennie was sure making a mess," Isaac said drily.

"They probably didn't have any supper."

Sim, too!

Everyone stuck up for that Bennie, Isaac told Sim, and was happy to see him nodding his head in agreement. "You have a point there."

Isaac was glad he had spoken. Sometimes schoolboys observed things from their lowly vantage point that adults like Sim would be wise to learn.

"You know if Barbara doesn't watch it, that little Bennie is going to be a handful, the way no one makes him listen," Isaac said.

Sim agreed.

Isaac was convinced Sim would make a great father. He was just humble enough, and agreeable, too. He took advice, and took it right. Yes, indeed, it would be a pure shame if Catherine and Sim never started dating.

On Friday, Ruthie stood by the blackboard, wringing her hands, her eyes clearly terrified as she lifted her head.

"I … h - h - h."

She stopped, searched for Isaac, found his face, then his eyes.

Come on, Ruthie! You can do this! He didn't say a word. His belief in her came from his eyes.

"H - hope m - m … my h …"

She stopped.

Isaac's eyes never left her face.

He was aware of Hannah and Calvin beside him. They all waited and waited. Ruthie took a deep breath. He watched as she clasped and unclasped her hands. That day, she spoke two whole sentences, haltingly, with exhausting effort.

At third recess, Isaac left sledding and found her sitting the porch, her feet dangling down the side.

"Ruthie, why don't we talk about your mam?"

he asked.

"Who told you?"

"Teacher Catherine."

"I told Hannah and Dora today. It feels good. It's … everything feels easier now."

Isaac grinned encouragingly. So she told him. The struggles at home, trying not to hate her mother, the relief now, knowing her problem may actually be physical.

The following Monday, Ruthie made real progress. Teacher Catherine was beside herself with excitement. The Christmas program was shaping into a good one, molded by days of practice, pleading, cajoling, praising, the teacher at the helm guiding her Christmas ship.

Isaac wondered if her energy and enthusiasm had all been because of Ruthie. He doubted it. Didn't Sim have something to do with it when he came to pick Isaac up Friday afternoon? Late on purpose, then yet. Teacher Catherine was sweeping the snow from the porch, her cheeks red, her eyes sparkling as they exchanged greetings.

Well, Isaac was done. They could just keep up all this nonsense. He was out of it.

If Sim wanted to wait on God, he could. Hadn't God always been slow? Look at Methuselah. He was 900 and some years old. Let Sim wait until they were both 60 and then they could go visit the eye doctor together. He was thoroughly tired of Sim's *ga-mach*. (way of doing things)

Christmas was coming, and the program and the spring wagon were much more important, anyway.

Chapter Ten

RUTHIE STOOD BY THE BLACKBOARD NOW, the only sign of agitation her interlaced fingers, which she loosened, then hung her arms at her side for only a second before entwining her fingers again.

Endlessly, they had practiced sentences, words that began with the letter B, or H, or C, the hardest ones.

Hannah and Dora spent nights at her house, listening to her amazing stories of the past when her mother had been ill.

Ruthie no longer picked her face. Her eyes seemed quieter, somehow.

The parents had their invitations to the Christmas program, stamped holly with brilliant red berries on a gold card, inviting them to Hickory Grove School at 1:00 P.M. on Friday, December 23.

One more day to practice, then two other schools were coming to see their program on Thursday, a day before the real one, when all the parents would attend.

The plays were shaping up. Four white sheets hung from the wires suspended from hooks in the walls and on the ceilings. Bright tinsel was draped from the curtains.

The poster was magnificent. It was the finest piece of freehand art work Hickory Grove School had ever shown. Isaac knew that, but didn't say so. It was bragging, which was wrong. It was a form of pride. He could be pleased with it, though; he just couldn't say so. He told Calvin, however, who said he agreed 100 percent. It was a great poster.

Teacher Catherine drew camels and wise men on the blackboard, and the upper-grade boys helped color them with colored chalk.

Isaac had to bite back his observance of the similarities between these camels and Hannah's horses on the poster. They looked exactly alike. The noses, especially.

Teacher Catherine's apron, even her *halsduch* (cape) was covered in colored chalk dust, but her blue eyes radiated her enthusiasm. She talked nonstop, even chewing gum at recess, which was sort of unusual. Chewing gum wasn't allowed in school.

Thursday morning, Isaac leaped out of bed, flicked the small blue lighter and lifted the glass lamp chimney on his kerosene lamp. The small flame traveled the length of the wick.

He yanked open his dresser drawer, hopped into his denim work trousers and shrugged into his blue shirt as shivers chased themselves across his cold shoulders.

It had to be zero degrees outside.

It was! The red mercury hovered at the zero, and if you stood on your toes and looked down, it was colder than zero degrees. No doubt Calvin would have the real temperature, though.

Isaac rushed through his chores. The minute he walked into the kitchen, Mam said he needed to shower before breakfast. His black Sunday pants and his green Christmas shirt were laid out. He was supposed to wear his good shoes, not his sneakers.

If Mam would give him time to catch his breath when he walked into the kitchen, it wouldn't be so bad. But barking orders when you were cold and hungry and wanted to sit by the coal stove and think of fried mush and dippy eggs just didn't work very well.

So Isaac grumbled under his breath, scalded himself in the shower and shivered into his Sunday clothes. He brushed his teeth, watching the blue foam from the Crest toothpaste splatter the mirror. His face looked pretty good this morning. He liked his green eyes. He thought they looked nice, but you couldn't tell people that. Not even Calvin.

He bowed his head over his plate. He had to rearrange his thoughts away from the Christmas program to thank God for his breakfast before digging into a pile of stewed saltine crackers, fried mush and dippy eggs. Now he felt much better, fueled to meet the day. Mam's eyes approved of his clean appearance, but nothing was said. It wasn't Mam's way.

"Did you get my name-exchange gift ready?" he asked Mam, as he bent to pull on his boots. His Sunday shoes were in his backpack, reminders of the importance of the day.

"Yes, indeed I did. Why would I wait till the day before the program?" she replied tartly.

Isaac laughed, knowing that was an insult. Mam prided herself on her good management.

The schoolhouse was fairly bursting at the seams, with Red Run and Oak Lane schools there at the same time. Teacher Catherine was flitting about, trying unsuccessfully to remain calm, unflappable.

Isaac could hardly wait to get started. This was Ruthie's chance to prove herself, and the SOS group's chance to savor their success. Isaac was confident, eager to get out there and show these schools what they had done.

The program went very well. The singing rose to the ceiling and swirled around the room, lighting on each pupil, bringing Christmas cheer to everyone.

Because the curtain divided the schoolroom, Isaac only became aware of Ruthie's absence when the program was almost over.

What had happened? Why had she failed to appear?

After "We Wish You a Merry Christmas" and the goodbye song were sung, the pupils of Hickory Grove rushed out the back door, one stream of exulting, yelling children, relieved to be free of restraint and tension.

Ruthie slunk along the side of the schoolhouse, her head bent, Hannah and Dora clustered around her. Isaac wasted no time.

"What happened, Ruthie?"

She shook her head. "I don't know."

Oh, boy.

There was nothing to say. Calvin and Michael's disappointment hung over their shoulders, a cape of black defeat.

Well, at least we won't expect her to say her poem tomorrow, Isaac thought. We failed. But it's only a Christmas poem.

Mam says acceptance of failure is a virtue, which is sort of hard to fathom, but I know now what she means, he thought. To lose with grace and dignity.

"Ruthie, it's okay," he told her, his voice kind.

She nodded.

"You want to practice?"

She looked at him, her eyes pools of fear. The monster called "I can't" had caught up with her.

The Hickory Grove pupils talked to some of the visiting school's children, only the ones they knew, who attended the same church services. The teachers soon herded the children into waiting vans, whisking them off to their own schools, allowing Teacher Catherine time to clean and prepare the classroom for the most important event of the Christmas season.

No matter how careful they had been, the upper-graders had erased parts of the camels' legs on the blackboard by leaning on the chalk tray in singing class. So Isaac and Calvin were put to work, filling in the erased spots.

Suddenly, Isaac was aware of Ruthie with a can of furniture polish and a dust cloth, viciously swiping desk tops, polishing them until they shone. In time to her ferocious swipes, she was singing, in jerks, but singing.

"I. Hope. My. Heart. Has. Heard." And on and on.

Isaac jabbed an elbow into Calvin's side, producing a puzzled expression and an "Ow!"

"Listen to Ruthie," Isaac hissed.

They stopped their work, their ears straining to the sound. They both knew it was her Christmas poem. Isaac shrugged his shoulders, turned to the blackboard and continued fixing the camels' legs. He was done with that SOS thing, same as he was done with Sim asking Catherine for a date. You could only do so much, and that was it. If Ruthie couldn't do it, then that was that. If Sim wanted to be a bachelor, then that was that, too.

He had other things in life to enjoy. Like a pony spring wagon. Imagine!

He told Calvin he might be getting one, which was a great surprise to Calvin, since Isaac's Christmas gifts usually amounted to less than half of his.

"What got into your dat?" he asked.

Isaac shrugged his shoulders, grinning happily.

At home, the house smelled of gingerbread, date and nut pudding, and chocolate, all mixed together in anticipation of Mam's Christmas dinner.

Dat brought home a whole quart of oysters for oyster stew on Christmas Eve. It was a tradition, to open gifts the evening before Christmas, and then savor the rich stew Mam made with that expensive jar of oysters. They only had oysters at Christmas-time.

The stale bread was brought from their freezer at the neighbor's garage and cut into cubes with the best bread knife to make *roasht*, that delicious holiday dish of bread cubes, celery, egg, and great chunks of turkey or chicken. Isaac was put to work chopping celery, the old wooden cutting board a sure prevention from cutting into Mam's countertop. He looked up when Sim came into the kitchen, sitting down to unlace his boots, humming softly under his breath.

"What are you doing?" Isaac asked, scooping up a handful of chopped celery.

"Oh, I might go watch the hockey players on Abner Speicher's pond for awhile."

"Is the pond fit?" Mam asked quickly.

"Should be."

"Not with 30 hockey players on it."

They went through this same conversation every year. Ice on the pond was a subject of great controversy, according to Mam. Six inches was sufficient, she'd say, until all those people started skating on top of it. Then what? She'd move around the kitchen wagging her head, finally giving in and saying if someone fell through the ice they would never forget it, and don't come crying to her, she'd tried to warn them.

"Wanna come along?" Sim asked Isaac.

Isaac jumped off his chair, raced around the kitchen searching for gloves, boots, and his coat, shouting his elation. Of course, he wanted to go!

He grabbed his hockey skates, clunked them into a corner of the *kessle-haus* (wash house) and raced back upstairs for an extra pair of socks.

His room was pitch-black. He groped on his night stand for his lighter, found it and flicked it on above his sock drawer. It took only a second until he located a pair of heavy wool socks and ran headlong down the stairs.

He didn't even think of Teacher Catherine. He didn't know girls came to these hockey games. He'd never been to one.

So when he saw Teacher Catherine sitting beside another girl he didn't know, warming her hands by the fire, he felt shy, unable to look at her.

Teachers belonged in a classroom, not at a hockey game.

"Hello, Isaac."

"Hello."

Quickly, he ducked his head as the other girl stared at him, smiling. He turned his back and prepared to pull on his skates. The schoolboys weren't allowed to play hockey with the big boys, but they had a small section of the pond roped off, and this was where Isaac was going as soon as he got his feet into his skates.

Sim's voice made him very still.

"Hello, Catherine. Kate." Sim nodded in the other girl's direction.

Well, no use hanging around. Sim wasn't going to do anything at all about having a date with Catherine anyway. So Isaac tiptoed on his skates through the snow, hit the ice and skated smoothly across the pond to Calvin and Michael.

What Isaac completely missed was the "King's Florist" truck that had crept slowly down Traverse Hill earlier that day, looking for Hickory Grove School.

And the brown-clad driver who hopped out with a gigantic poinsettia in a lovely, woven basket trailing dark green ivy, with a Christmas card inserted on a plastic spike that said, "Merry Christmas, Catherine. A friend, Simon Stoltzfus."

He never knew his teacher pulled out the plastic spike, tore at the card with trembling fingers, her face tense with unanswered questions.

He didn't see her read the words for only a second, then fling the card to her desk, crumple into a second-grader's desk and laugh and cry at the same time, then get up and whirl between the desks until her skirt billowed out, aflight with genuine happiness.

Isaac had been at home chopping celery.

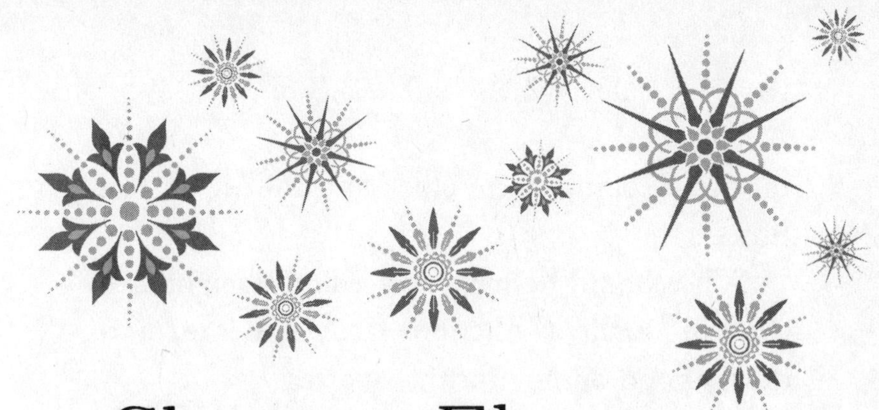

Chapter Eleven

ISAAC WAS STIFF, SORE AND EXTREMELY TIRED at 5:00 a.m. when his cheap, plastic alarm began its nerve-wracking little beeps. It was one of the dumbest alarm clocks anyone had ever invented for five dollars at Walmart. Mam could at least have picked a better color.

His hand groped for the too-small button that shut off the hysterical beeping, gave up and threw it against the wall. When he remembered this was the day of the Christmas program, he retrieved the still-beeping alarm clock and shut it off this time.

Why should he have noticed any heightened color in Teacher Catherine's face? Or her extraordinary good humor, for that matter?

It was Christmas, after all. The program had gone well yesterday, and today was the season's crowning glory, with parents, friends and relatives cramming into the schoolhouse, craning their necks to see better.

Mam had brushed his coat well and washed his green Christmas shirt and hung it by the coal stove in the kitchen to dry until morning. She had polished his Sunday shoes and hung out his black Sunday vest. He felt very fine, wearing all those Sunday clothes.

Calvin looked fancy, he thought, wearing a red shirt with a hint of plaid design in it. Michael wore a green shirt, with a swirl in the pattern of the fabric. Isaac's was a plain, flat-out green. The girls wore red or green, but he couldn't remember who wore what.

Teacher Catherine looked especially fine. She wore a festive red dress, her usual black apron, Sunday shoes, and a very new white covering that looked just a bit better than the ordinary ones she wore on weekdays.

Isaac guessed playing baseball was what really got those coverings wrinkled and brown, the way the covering strings flapped and fluttered behind those girls dashing to first base. When they went sledding, the coverings stayed in the cloakroom in a Tupperware container, the girls throwing head scarves of rainbow hues on their heads and tying them below their chins, jutting out their faces to secure them firmly.

Isaac had a small black plastic comb in his vest pocket, which he used repeatedly throughout the forenoon. He wanted to appear neat and orderly, showing his green eyes to their best advantage.

They exchanged their gifts in the forenoon since the program didn't start until 1:00. Isaac had Henry's name and was proud to see how pleased Henry looked to find two Lewis B. Miller books and a pair of heavy gloves in his package.

Hannah had Isaac's name. He received a picture of howling wolves, an LED headlamp—he had three at home—and a package of Dentyne chewing gum. He was pleased. The howling wolves were cool. You could always chew gum or use another headlamp. Isaac thanked Hannah, and she ducked her head and wouldn't answer. He should have been nicer about those horses on the poster.

Teacher Catherine presented each of the boys with a small cedar chest with horses decoupaged on the lid. It was one of the neatest things Isaac had ever owned. When he opened the lid, the contents took his breath away. It was full of root beer barrels! His absolute favorite! He thanked her fervently, and Teacher Catherine's eyes twinkled at him. He thought her the most wonderful person he had ever met.

The big girls were each given a hand-carved, wooden mirror with a lovely, smooth, rounded handle. Ruthie said it was a *hinna-gook schpickel.*

(mirror to look behind you.) Calvin and Michael said their sisters all had one on their dressers, and they worked great to get your fighter fish going crazy. That really got Isaac's attention. A fighter fish? What was that?

Michael had a small aquarium in his room. It was rectangular, filled with smooth stones and plastic plants, but it contained only one grayish-red fighter fish. The reason they had to live alone was because they were so angry they killed any other fish that was in the aquarium. They swam around thinking they were the boss, always. But if you held up one of those *hinna gook schpikla* and the fish caught sight of himself, he instantly propelled himself into a frenzy, slamming against the side of the aquarium repeatedly.

Isaac listened, amazed. That was really something.

Hannah said that was cruel, then turned up her nose, inhaled mightily and stalked off.

Dora agreed.

Sarah said at least the fish had a bit of excitement in its life, swimming around like that all by itself.

Isaac informed her fish couldn't think.

Dora asked, how did he know?

Calvin said if you read about fish in the encyclopedia you could know.

Ruthie didn't say anything. Isaac looked at her and smiled. He thought that was a good quality, staying quiet the way she did. For a girl, anyway.

The little boys got wildlife books from Teacher Catherine. Big hardcover ones. With the longest Reese's Peanut Butter Cup Isaac had ever seen.

The little girls each received a pretty little chest, white, with a lid that opened and was lined with pink or lavender. It played music if you opened it. There was a handkerchief and a tiny, sparkly bag of red and silver Hershey's Kisses inside. Isaac thought Teacher Catherine must be rich, the way she spent money for Christmas.

All the children were agitated, the impending program, and the exchange of Christmas gifts goading them on. They raced outside to the playground, and then talked too much and far too loudly in the classroom. Before lunchtime, quite a few of the pupils had forgotten to put their foil-wrapped food on the propane gas heater. Little Sally cried, wanting her pizza warmed, so Teacher Catherine put her arm around the little girl's waist and pulled her close, then turned the heater up as far as it would go, heating her lunch in five minutes.

No one was really very hungry, although they did their best to hide that fact. Nervous fingers pressed sandwiches flat, bits of iceberg lettuce were torn to shreds and finally stuffed back into plastic sandwich bags. Apples were put back into the colorful Rubbermaid lunch boxes, with only a few bites missing. Pretzels stuck in dry throats.

The boys spent a great deal of time in the horse shed, their shoulders hunched as they rammed their hands in their pockets, shifting their weight from one foot to the other, talking nonsensical things, laughing nervously about things that really weren't that funny.

They all heard the arrival of the first horse and buggy. The unmistakable rumbling of steel-rimmed wheels on macadam, accompanied by the dull clopping of a fast-paced driving horse.

The boys beat it to the schoolhouse porch, a flock of nervous black-clad boys like frightened starlings. It was Levi Stoltzfuses already. It was barely 12:00. The program wasn't scheduled to begin until 1:00.

The boys moved in a huddle to the side of the porch as the team pulled up to the steps.

The buggy door opened, and Levi *sei* Rachel stepped down lightly, holding her baby wrapped in a blue blanket.

"*Vit mit da Dat Koinma*?" she asked. (Want to come with Dad?) The little boy clinging to the glove compartment nodded, and the buggy moved off.

Rachel was holding the diaper bag, the baby, and a large plastic container.

Isaac stepped forward. "*Brauchtsh hilf*?" (Do

you need help?)

Rachel nodded gratefully. "*Denke.*" (Thank you.)

Proudly, Isaac carried the red container, lowering his eyes to look through the clear plastic lid. Chocolate-covered something! Oh, the wonderful things mothers brought to the Christmas program!

There were plates of cookies and trays of bars and cupcakes and homemade candy. Potato chips and pretzels and cheese. Party mix and popcorn, mounds of tortillas spread with cream cheese and seasonings, crammed full of ham and cheese, cut in little pinwheels of pure pleasure. There were paper cups of fruit punch, iced tea, coffee and hot chocolate.

No one thought of healthy food at Christmastime.

Isaac was always pleased with Mam's contribution. She was a fine baker. This year she made extra peanut-butter tartlets for the Christmas program, which made Isaac especially glad. They were a buttery, rich crust shaped into miniature muffin tins, with a small Reese's cup pressed into them. Calvin and Michael loved them.

Second-grader Sally spied her mother and moved to her side quickly, reaching for her little brother Jesse, bursting to show her classmates how cute he was, what a capable helper she was, uncovering his face, pulling on the strings of his pale blue stocking cap as her friends watched enviously.

Isaac's heart began to race in earnest when a white 15-passenger van slowed, then turned into the snow covered driveway.

Fremme! (Strangers!)

The boys jostled each other from their elevated position on the porch, then stood respectfully, watching. A few young girls hopped down, then turned to open the second door, allowing more room for the remaining passengers.

Doddy and Mommy Stoltzfus! (Grandpa and Grandma) Isaac was pink cheeked with high spirits. What a treat!

It was interesting to see who the people were that had to hire a driver, living too far away for their horse and buggy to bring them. Isaac knew Doddy Stoltzfuses lived in *die unna Beckveh* (lower Pequea) which was below Kirkwood and Quarryville, very seldom making the long drive to Gordonville.

It took awhile for Mommy to step down. She had to go backwards, grasping the arm of the second seat. Her black shawl and bonnet and the lower half of her skirt were the only things visible, as Doddy guided her feet to the running board of the van, then handed her the wooden cane with the black rubber tip she always used.

She grasped his hand as he steered her to the porch steps. His wide black hat brim hid his face, and only his white beard was visible in sharp contrast against his *ivva-ruck*. (overcoat)

"*Boova*!" (Boys) he said, as he maneuvered Mommy past them.

"Hello!" Mommy said, smiling widely, as she followed Doddy through the schoolhouse door.

There were other grandparents and aunts and uncles Isaac did not know. The van emptied itself one by one, everyone clad in the usual black. The boys greeted each visitor politely, then unanimously decided it was too cold on the porch, when, really, they were simply curious.

Teacher Catherine's face looked a shade whiter now, her mouth a grim line. That put fear in Isaac's own heart. Would everything go well? Would they remember their parts? Steely resolve replaced the fear. Of course, they would. Hadn't they practiced endlessly? They all knew their parts backward and forward, didn't they? It was like a repetition now. They said their parts without thinking very much at all.

Yes, everything would go well.

More teams turned in and unloaded their occupants. Little preschoolers followed their mothers up the steps, their eyes wide with curiosity, shyness mixed with anticipation.

Teacher Catherine's desk had been pushed to the back of the classroom, so that was where mothers deposited their offerings of Christmas treats. Fathers carried large five-gallon plastic orange containers of tea and punch, and one marked "ice water." Rectangular green coffee urns were brought in. Some mothers hurried over to make sure no spigot leaked, and put a few paper towels beneath them to catch any drips.

Isaac thought mothers must be the same, every last one of them. What did it matter if coffee dripped on the tile floor?

The whole classroom looked as if a hurricane blew through it after a Christmas program. He had seen it often enough. It never failed: half a dozen of those little preschoolers–who were never properly supervised–spilled their fruit punch. The other children ran through the sticky liquid before mothers–who talked entirely too much–saw it, leaving Teacher Catherine to clean up the whole unbelievable mess by herself.

A few weeks ago, Isaac would have tried to get Sim to stay and help Teacher Catherine clean up. Wouldn't that be an excellent opportunity to ask someone for a date?

But he had moved on. He no longer cared. If Sim wanted to be a bachelor and think himself a prophet, then he'd just have to do that. Isaac's services were over.

He looked at the clock.

12:45.

His pulse accelerated. He felt a bit skittish inside.

He needed to find Ruthie. Even a shot in the dark was better than no shot at all.

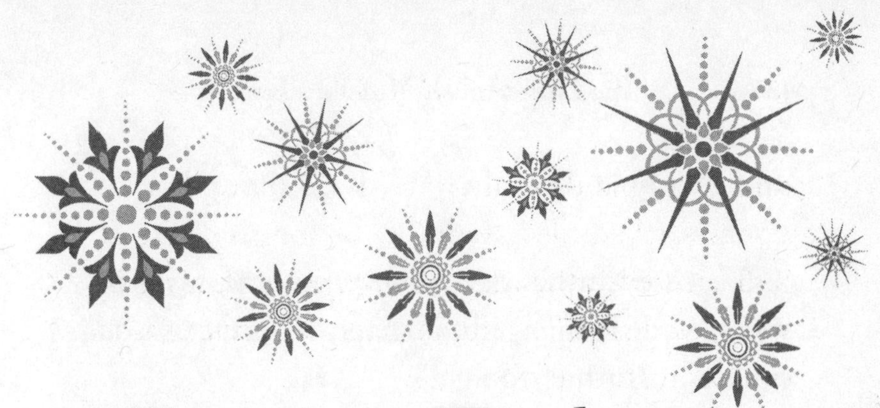

Chapter Twelve

He found Ruthie in the cloakroom, standing by the window with Hannah, watching the teams pull up to the door.

He caught sight of Sam, Dat's superb black Standardbred driving horse. So they were here.

"Ruthie."

She looked over at Isaac, her eyebrows lifted.

"You going to do it?"

She took a deep breath. Her shoulders squared visibly. She looked straight into Isaac's eyes and said clearly and firmly, "Yes, Isaac, I'm going to do it."

Isaac's eyebrows danced way up, and his grin was so wide it changed the shape of his face. "You can do it, Ruthie! You go!"

She nodded, her face a picture of radiance. What had happened? Gone was the hand-wringing, the miserable expression.

Well, same as with Sim and Catherine, he wasn't going to expect too much. Stay levelheaded. Expect her to do it, but accept failure if it came.

The classroom was filling up now. Church benches had replaced the Ping-Pong table in the middle, which had been placed along the side of the room. The cloakroom was piled high with coats, bonnets and shawls. Babies cried. Mothers hushed them nervously, hoping they would fall asleep, or at the very least, remain quiet with some toys or a graham cracker.

Fathers held on to squirming little boys, bending to whisper words of discipline. "*Bleib sitza.*" (Stay sitting.)

A steady hum of voices, laughter, greetings, a kaleidoscope of faces, white coverings, colorful dresses, shirts accentuated with black vests. English people came to the program, too. Vans came, bringing friends of Teacher Catherine, friends of parents, all seated side by side, their colorful coats in stark contrast to the black.

Teacher Catherine herded the children into their curtained-off square of space. She spoke a few words of encouragement, made sure the necessary items for the plays were all in order and warned them all to be absolutely quiet behind the curtain.

"Do you want the windows up or down?" she asked.

"Down!" everyone whispered.

"It gets too warm in here."

"Too many people."

"Put them down."

Teacher Catherine nodded, smiled and said, "Do your best."

1:00. She tapped a small bell. The signal to begin!

Total silence now, as faces strained eagerly toward the open space in front of the blackboard, their stage.

The pupils sang a resounding chorus of Christmas songs first, the 21 beautiful voices blending into that special innocent harmony that only children can produce.

The emotional individuals in the audience sniffed, lifting spectacles to wipe eyes with meticulously ironed Sunday handkerchiefs.

Isaac stood in the back row between Ruthie and Hannah, singing with all his might. He knew their singing was good. In the guest book they passed to visitors to sign their names, almost all of them praised their singing. Isaac didn't like Hannah much, but she could sing. Her voice carried well with Isaac's, although he'd never tell her. Likely she'd take it as an insult.

After the singing, the smallest boy in school welcomed the audience to the Christmas program.

Standing all alone, his head lifted high, his voice carrying well, he said clearly,

I'm very small, and very scared,
But this job I have to do:
Welcome you all on this glad day,
Plus, "Merry Christmas," too!

Smiling shyly, he turned on his heel and hurried behind the curtain.

There was a skit after that. Second, third and fourth grades came onstage with their skates and winter clothing.

Isaac's poem followed. He stood straight and tall and spoke in his usual crisp voice that carried well. His poem had 14 verses, which streamed from him effortlessly.

He spied Sim, lounging along the back wall in his red shirt, a head taller than his friend Abner. So he was here. Good.

Laughter followed the humorous parts. Babies became restless, were taken outside or given to another person.

The Abraham Lincoln play went well. Ruthie spoke with confidence, using her best voice, with Isaac supporting her.

The play about the wise men was flubbed a bit when Matthew forgot to finish his lines, confusing Rebecca, who bravely soldiered on, acting as if nothing out of the ordinary had happened. Good for her!

The first-graders wouldn't hold still behind the curtain, so Isaac snapped Ephraim's suspenders and shot them all a vicious glance, which did wonders. The little chap was always the one who stirred up everyone else. Like Bennie, probably no one made him listen at home.

The upper graders sang two German songs, "*Stille Nacht*" (Silent Night) and "*Kommet Alle*" (Come All).

That was always touching for Dat. Being conservative, he was touched by the continual teaching of German in the schools. He fervently hoped that the *Muttasproch* (mother language) of the forefathers would not be neglected and that the old, but precious, tradition would be kept. So when these young people sang the old hymns in the beloved language, it meant much to him, and his respect for Teacher Catherine was heightened.

Isaac saw Mam lift her glasses, unobtrusively extending a forefinger to wipe the wetness that had pooled beneath one eye.

Little, first-grade Daniel's part was to sit in a Christmas cake, accidentally, of course, while wearing an extra pair of pants, of course, which was always funny. The classroom erupted into unabashed laughter. Very loud, Isaac thought, which was good.

A soft footfall, and he heard Ruthie. Isaac froze. Chills chased themselves up his back. He became warm all over. Her voice was strong. The words came slowly, but they were absolutely distinct. He caught Calvin's eye. Calvin shook his head in disbelief. From the first line to the very end of her poem, she spoke without faltering, her voice rising and falling in time to the beauty of the words.

No one in the audience knew there was anything unusual about the fact that Lloyd Allgyer's Ruthie spoke her whole poem slowly and clearly.

Only the SOS group and Teacher Catherine, who were bursting with Christmas joy.

The hour and 15 minutes flew by, as the plays and poems mixed with singing filled up everyone's senses. The spirit of Christmas swirled about and infused everyone who was in the room. Many of the guests were sorry to hear the closing song, telling each other it had been an outstanding program this year, that someone had spent a lot of time putting all this into the students.

Amid hearty hand-clapping from the audience, the pupils poured out of the back door into the clear cold air, relieved of the pressure to perform well, relieved of the month of practice, the hard work of memorizing and delivering the lines just right.

The upper-graders were pulled to Ruthie as if a gigantic magnet's force drew them there. Hannah and Dora hugged her and squealed high and long. Isaac found that a bit overboard, but what else could you expect from girls?

"Ruthie! You did it!" Calvin yelled.

Isaac wanted to know how. "How could you do that?"

They all huddled together in the cold, cold air, as Ruthie crossed her arms tightly around her waist to stay warmer and keep from shivering. She told them she had practiced in front of a mirror, over and over and over, finally grasping the concept of speaking slower. "When I stutter, I'm afraid I can't say it, so I go too fast. Sort of like someone falling down the stairs. When they feel themselves slipping, they go too far in the opposite direction to stop themselves and roll down the stairs."

They all laughed about that description, which surprised Ruthie, who joined in whole- heartedly. It was a dose of Christmas spirit multiplied by 10, all brought about by Ruthie's success. It felt good.

Teacher Catherine met them inside the door, gathered Ruthie into her arms and held her there.

Only the upper-graders knew why. Isaac felt his nostrils sting with emotion, but shook his head to straighten his hair, then looked out the window and blinked furiously. He got out his little black comb and pulled it through his hair, very hard, to get rid of that teary feeling.

They had to wait in line to fill their plates. Mothers bent over little ones grasping paper plates teetering dangerously with cookies and potato chips. Everyone was talking at once. Smiles were everywhere, faces shining with good humor.

Teacher Catherine moved among her pupils, thanking, congratulating, praising their efforts. Her face was absolutely radiant. Isaac could tell her praise was genuine. She was so pleased. That made it all worthwhile.

Finally, he reached the stack of paper plates. He helped himself to a large square of Rice Krispie Treats, pushed it to one side of his plate and added a monster cookie, three chocolate- covered Ritz crackers with peanut butter, a large scoop of Chex Mix and three or four of Mam's tarts. He was ravenously hungry. He had been too nervous to eat much of his food at lunchtime.

First he ate the monster cookie. Every year, Ben Zook *sei* Annie made these cookies. They were rough-textured with oatmeal and loaded with red and green M & M's for Christmas, of course. They were soft and chewy and buttery and perfect, every time.

Calvin was chomping on a handful of Chex Mix, sounding like a horse munching oats, spilling a lot of it on the floor, too hungry to worry about the excess.

Michael ate whoopie pies, one after the other, as fast as he could cram them into his mouth. Icing clung to his chin and the side of his mouth, but he didn't seem to mind, until his sister came bustling over with a handful of napkins and told him to wipe his mouth, and where were his manners? She had her eyebrows in that position, the one that meant he had overstepped his boundaries, and if he didn't straighten up it would go all the way to the Supreme Court named Mam.

Michael kicked carelessly in her direction and told her to mind her own business, he could take care of himself. Isaac giggled behind his Rice Krispie Treat.

Then Dan Glick brought the propane lamp stand out for Teacher Catherine, followed by Aaron Fisher who carried the propane tank and accessories. The lamp stand was made of cherry with a magazine rack on one side. It was beautiful.

Catherine put both hands to her mouth, her blue eyes opened wide and she said nothing at all for awhile. When the women crowded around, she began thanking them, saying it was too much, just way too much.

Dat went around with an envelope, collecting the money from each family.

Twenty-eight dollars. That wasn't bad, they said.

Who made the cabinet? they asked.

Sol King?

Oh, he was one of the best.

Wasn't that cherry wood different, now?

Did Teacher Catherine have other cherry pieces?

Levi *sei* Rachel thought her bedroom suit was cherry, but she wasn't sure.

The women nodded their heads, pleased. It was a good choice. Teacher Catherine was worth it, that was one thing sure. She had such a nice way with the children, didn't she?

The blanketed horses were becoming restless, stomping their feet in the snow at their stand where they were tied to the board fence. Mothers collected gifts, stashed them in bags or leftover cardboard boxes, and herded their children into their coats.

Fathers carried the boxes and empty trays and containers, stuffing them under buggy seats, as children clambered in, still munching that last piece of chocolate.

Doddy Stoltzfus pulled at Isaac's sleeve. "Isaac, *vee bisht?*" (How are you?)

"*Goot. Goot!*" Isaac answered, grinning happily.

"You did good!" High praise from Doddy. Isaac grinned, basking in the kind words from his grandfather.

Sim walked up, extending his hand, greeting Doddy. Doddy beamed as he lifted his head to meet Sim's eyes.

Isaac walked away, irked at Sim. Sim would be as old as Doddy and still would never have asked Teacher Catherine for a date.

Oh, well.

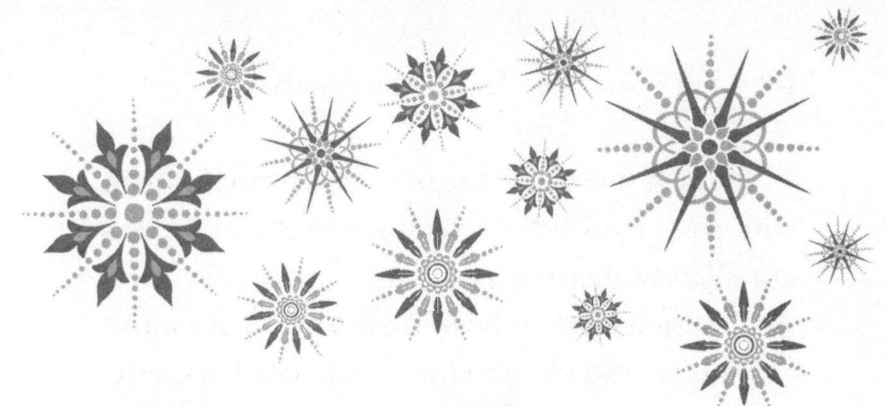

Chapter Thirteen

Dat and Mam were one of the last ones to leave. Sim, of course, the now deeply entrenched bachelor, was one of the first to hitch up his horse and head home.

Mam bustled about the classroom like a puffed-up little biddy hen, clucking about the mess. She had no idea this is what it looked like after a program. My goodness!

Catherine seemed a bit flustered, her cheeks about the color of her dress, but she remained polite, laughing frequently.

Mam noticed the gorgeous poinsettia, asking who gave it to her. "Oh, someone," was Catherine's answer, same as she told her pupils when they clustered about her desk in the usual way.

So Isaac rode home slouched in the back seat, his eyelids becoming heavy, rocked to a blissful state by the motion of the buggy.

It was all over now. He could relax and look forward to the Christmas dinner at home. He'd do his chores, then make himself comfortable with one of Calvin's books.

Dat talked to Mam about the singing. He'd never heard a school sing better. It must be that Catherine had a *gaub* (talent) in bringing out the best in her pupils. Mam said yes, it wasn't often you heard something like that. It seemed the children put their heart into it, didn't they?

Isaac grinned, wondering if they forgot he was in the back seat.

Back at the schoolhouse, a lone buggy retraced its steps, the horse a high-stepping sorrel Saddlebred, his ears bent forward in the typical heart-shaped fashion.

Sim got out slowly, led Fred into the buggy shed, slipped the neck rope around his neck and knotted the rope securely in the ring attached to the wall. After throwing a blanket over the horse's back, he wiped down the front of his coat before striding purposefully to the front door.

Teacher Catherine was pouring hot water from the kettle on the stove into a plastic scrub bucket, when she heard a knock.

Was it a knock?

She froze, then tried to get ahold of her fear. It was still broad daylight; no one was going to hurt her; no one knew she was here; it was the Christmas season; she would be fine.

With her heart beating heavily, her eyes wide, a hand to her throat, she answered the knock. She couldn't think of one word to say, so she didn't say anything at all. She just stood there and looked at Sim Stoltzfus, all six feet of him, and thought there was simply no reason for him to be there.

"I thought maybe you would appreciate a bit of help," he said.

She looked into his green eyes and could form no words, so she stood aside and ushered him in.

Sim whistled, soft and low.

"What a mess!"

"Yeah." She had found her voice. "If you don't mind, you could burn the trash."

"Sure."

Eagerly, he grabbed the plastic garbage bags.

She added a dollop of Pine-Sol to the warm water in the plastic bucket, while trying to calm her racing heart.

Sim came back and took over with the mop, shedding his coat as he spoke. She watched him with large blue eyes and wondered if she should say something about the poinsettia or wait until he mentioned it first.

She began unpinning the curtains, taking them down. He talked of everyday, mundane things that put her at ease in a surprising way.

He said it was a shame to erase the camels and wise men, but she said she was glad to do it. There was a time for everything, and she was glad the Christmas program was over, that it was a lot of work.

Sim nodded his head and watched her stretching to reach the pins that held the curtains to the wire. He told her she was a bit too short for the job and proceeded to help.

That was when her heart went all crazy again, and she could hardly breathe. She became so flustered she went out and swept the porch. When she returned, he had folded the sheets and was back to mopping floors.

He talked about the program, then asked why everyone was hugging the one eighth-grade girl. What was her name? Ruthie? He leaned against the wall and held the mop handle, while she forgot herself and launched into a vivid account of Ruthie overcoming her stuttering problem, the SOS group, and the grand way she had grasped the concept of speaking slowly.

Sim watched her face, the way she moved her hands when she spoke, and knew this was the girl he wanted to marry and live with for the remainder of his days.

When he finished mopping the floor, they moved the teacher's desk back to the front of the room. They washed the blackboard. Catherine stood back admiring the smooth blackness of it.

They found two containers of cookies someone had forgotten, so they sat by the teacher's desk and ate.

Sim asked her what she thought of the poinsettia. He watched her lovely face light up, listened to her blushing thanks.

She said, "You shouldn't have."

"I wanted to let you know I was your friend."

"Thank you. It was nice of you to remember me."

Sim's one eyebrow lifted.

"Remember you? I never stop thinking about you, so how could I remember you?"

He laughed easily when she became flustered.

Then he became very sober. The classroom was silent. The winter sunlight was fading fast as the sun became veiled by cold gray clouds, then slid behind Elam's windmill, putting it in stark contrast to the evening light.

Out on Route 340, a diesel engine shifted gears. The cry of a flock of crows echoed across the stubbles of the cornfields as an approaching horse and buggy chased them off. A child cried out at the adjacent farm, all sounds of a thriving community, lives interwoven, a reed basket of old traditions and new ways, yet so much remained the same.

For hundreds of years, young men had sought God's leading in asking for a young girl's hand. The world turned on its axis, and life was continually reinvented. New hopes, new dreams, a young man seeking a worthy companion, someone to love, to share their lives, the cycle was still moving from seed to harvest, to every season under the sun.

And so Sim found the God-given courage to tell her what was on his mind and in his heart.

"I know I don't stand much of a chance, but I won't have any rest until I ask. Will you accept my offer of friendship? Will you allow me to take you to the Christmas supper on Sunday evening?" Catherine sat very still, her hands folded in her lap, her head bowed.

As long as Sim lived, he carried the sight of her face as she lifted it to the sun's last rays, her brilliantly blue eyes holding a light of gladness. Before she spoke he knew. And when she spoke, he carried the remembrance of her words in his heart always.

"Oh my, Sim Stoltzfus."

Then, she laughed, a soft, happy sound.

"Yes."

That was all she said.

When he helped her into the buggy, he wanted to crush her light form to his, but he didn't. He could wait. Sitting beside her in the coziness of the buggy's lap robe was more than enough. He was blessed beyond anything he deserved.

He held her hand much longer than was necessary when he helped her from the buggy. Was it just his own craziness, or did her hand linger as well?

That evening, in the barn, Isaac was tired, grumpy and in a hurry to finish the chores. He had no time for Sim. When Sim asked him to take the baler twine to the burn barrel, Isaac said no, Sim could do it himself.

Dat heard him and said sternly, "Go, Isaac."

So that was the reason Isaac had nothing to do with Sim at the supper table. Life wasn't fair, when you were the youngest son. You always had to do what no one else wanted to do. Just being the smallest made everyone naturally assume it was his chore.

Taking out Mam's slop pail from under the sink, for instance. That vile little plastic ice cream bucket with a lid on it, setting there for days with apple peelings and cold, congealed oatmeal or Cream-of-Wheat, bacon grease, and spoiled peaches. No one had to smell it except the person taking it out and dumping it in the hog's trough.

His Christmas spirit was all used up, fizzled out, sputtered, and cold.

There was potato soup for supper, on top of all life's other atrocities. And the potato soup had hard-boiled eggs in it, which made him shiver. Gross.

Sim acted as if the potato soup was the finest thing Mam had ever cooked, opening his mouth wide to shovel the filled spoon into it.

Isaac ate bread-and-butter pickles, then felt slightly sick to his stomach. He swallowed hard when Sim cleared his throat and asked Dat if it was proper to bring Catherine to the Christmas dinner.

Dat looked up, surprised.

Mam's spoon stopped halfway to her mouth, then resumed slowly.

"Since we're dating now, I wondered if you'd object?"

"You're …? What?" Dat said.

"I asked Teacher Catherine."

Dat smiled, Mam became all flustered and teary, and Dat nodded soberly and said he guessed it would be all right. Then he tried to look stern, but failed completely.

Isaac's mouth fell open.

"Did you ask her?"

"Yes, Isaac, I did. She said yes."

Isaac said nothing at all.

Later though, he said a lot. He said it to Sim, his Christmas spirit flaming brightly as he congratulated Sim in the best way he knew how. He hit him in the back of his head with a snowball, then took off running, Mam's plastic slop pail abandoned in a snowdrift, where Catherine found it in the spring.

The End

Christmas Reflection

I hope my heart has heard the song
The shepherds heard that night.
I hope my heart has found the star
The wise men kept in sight.
Then maybe I will find my way
To the quiet manger, too.
So my heart can kneel in worship,
Bringing gifts sincere and true.

About the Author

Linda Byler was raised in an Amish family and is an active member of the Amish church today. Growing up, Linda loved to read and write. In fact, she still does. Linda is well-known within the Amish community as a columnist for a weekly Amish newspaper.

Linda is the author of the *Lizzie Searches for Love* series, as well as *Sadie's Montana*, which includes the novels *Wild Horses*, *Keeping Secrets*, and *The Disappearances*. She is also the author of *Lizzie's Amish Cookbook: Favorite recipes from three generations of Amish cooks*!

More Books by Linda Byler

Available from your favorite bookstore or online retailer.

"Author Linda Byler is Amish, which sets this book apart both in the rich details of Amish life and in the lack of melodrama over disappointments and tragedies. Byler's writing will leave readers eager for the next book in the series."
—*Publishers Weekly* review of *Wild Horses*

Sadie's Montana

BOOK ONE

BOOK TWO

BOOK THREE

Lizzie Searches for Love

BOOK ONE

BOOK TWO

BOOK THREE

COOKBOOK